MIDSUMMER NIGHT IN THE WORKHOUSE

First published in Great Britain in 2011 by Persephone Books

This edition published in 2011 by
House of Anansi Press Inc.
110 Spadina Avenue, Suite 801
Toronto, ON, M5V 2K4
Tel. 416-363-4343
Fax 416-363-1017
www.anansi.ca

Distributed in Canada by
HarperCollins Canada Ltd.
1995 Markham Road
Scarborough, ON, M1B 5M8
Toll free tel. 1-800-387-0117

Distributed in the United States by
Publishers Group West
1700 Fourth Street
Berkeley, CA 94710
Toll free tel. 1-800-788-3123

House of Anansi Press is committed to protecting our natural environment. As part of our efforts, the interior of this book is printed on paper that contains 100% post-consumer recycled fibres, is acid-free, and is processed chlorine-free.

15 14 13 12 11   1 2 3 4 5

LIBRARY AND ARCHIVES CANADA CATALOGUING IN PUBLICATION

Athill, Diana
Midsummer night in the workhouse / Diana Athill.

Short stories.
ISBN 978-1-77089-061-9

I. Title.

PR6051.T43M54 2011   823'.914   C2011-903976-1

Library of Congress Control Number: 2011929923

Cover design: Alysia Shewchuk
Text design and typesetting: Keystroke, Tettenhall, Wolverhampton

Canada Council   Conseil des Arts
for the Arts   du Canada

ONTARIO ARTS COUNCIL
CONSEIL DES ARTS DE L'ONTARIO

We acknowledge for their financial support of our publishing program the Canada Council for the Arts, the Ontario Arts Council, and the Government of Canada through the Canada Book Fund.

Printed and bound in Canada

MIDSUMMER NIGHT IN THE WORKHOUSE

by

DIANA ATHILL

with a new preface by

THE AUTHOR

ANANSI
INTERNATIONAL

CONTENTS

PREFACE

I can remember in detail being hit by my first story one January morning in 1958. Until that moment I had been hand-maiden, as editor, to other people's writing, without ever dreaming of myself as a writer. Then, at nine o'clock one sunny morning, I was taking my Pekinese across the Outer Circle of Regent's Park when a car pulled up and its driver beckoned. I thought he was going to ask the way somewhere, but what he said was: 'I am Mustafa Ali from Istanbul – will you come and have coffee with me?' At nine in the morning – what an optimist! I thought as I went on my way, laughing; and how odd that someone who looked so very like a man I'd once known, a diamond merchant from Cape Town called Marcel, should behave in such a Marcellish way. And I began to remember Marcel.

All through that day Marcel kept popping up in my head, and with him came an oddly gleeful sensation of energy. When I got home from the office I thought: 'I know what – I'm going to write a story about him,' and down I sat at my typewriter. Soon, however, it became obvious that a story about Marcel would be have to be set in the diamond trade, about which I knew too little, so that idea was no good . . . but the energy sensation was still strongly there. And then, suddenly, another man from the past loomed up, and I knew for certain that he was the one, and that I was going to get him down exactly as he was. Which I did, and the story is 'An Unavoidable Delay'.

As soon as that story was finished, another one began, and by the end of the year I had written nine. I did not think about them in advance: a feeling would brew up, a first sentence would occur to me, and then the story would come, as though it had been there all the time. Sometimes it would turn into 'work' halfway through and I would have to cast about for the conclusion to which the story must be brought, but more often it finished itself. Some of them connected very closely with my own experience, some of them, to my astonishment, depended on it so slightly that they might almost have been 'invented' (the 'invented' ones were the ones of which I felt most proud, but, with one exception, the others were better).

Although the first story, 'An Unavoidable Delay', was exciting to write, it was not to be my thunder-clap one. That role was to be played by the third of the nine I wrote in quick succession before coming to the end of them. At the start of 1958, the *Observer* announced a prize to be given for a story called 'The Return', 3000 words long. My third story was to be called something else, but 'The Return' would fit it fairly well. It was a hundred words too long, but one of the things editing had taught me is that you can always cut, so chop-chop, change the title, and off it went under the required pseudonym for which I chose 'Mister What', having just won a fiver on a horse of that name in the Grand National. That story won First Prize.

This would have been stunning however it had happened, and was made almost unbearably blissful by the fact that in the eight months between submitting it and hearing the news I had forgotten all about it, and that when the prize (£500, big money in those days) was handed over, they told me there had been 2000 entries.

You do not look up because you know that you cannot climb the tree. You have forgotten, by now, that there is fruit hidden among its leaves. Then, suddenly, without a puff of wind, a great velvety peach falls plump into your hand. It happens to other people, perhaps; it never happens to oneself . . . I am still licking peach juice off my fingers. . . . Bury me, dear friends, with a copy of the *Observer* folded under my head, for it was the *Observer*'s prize that woke me up to the fact that I could write and had become happy.

In André Deutsch Ltd, our publishing firm, the belief that short stories by unknown writers were publishing poison was so deeply entrenched that I never thought of offering my stories to a British publisher. Some of them did get into magazines, and into an anthology, but the best thing that happened to them was that a dear man called Ken, a director of Doubleday's in New York whose surname has been lost through a hole in my geriatric head, fell in love with them. I assumed that his colleagues allowed Ken a folly every now and then, and that publishing my stories was one of them: certainly they never earned their very modest advance. They caused no stir (even that prize seemed to be noticed by very few people apart from my friends) so seeing them here, charmingly presented by Persephone, amazes as much as it delights me.

Do they deserve this honour? Reading them now I enjoy them, but that may well be because they recall the special flavour of the thrill you experience when first you make things happen with words on paper: the discovery that I could write changed my life for the better in a very profound way, so they mean a great deal to me. How I hope they will give pleasure to those who meet them for the first time in their new and elegant dress.

Diana Athill
Highgate, 2010

MIDSUMMER NIGHT IN THE WORKHOUSE

THE REAL THING

I went to the dance with Thomas Toofat. It's Toogood really, but he *is* too fat, with frizzy hair and flat feet. We never meant to let him know we call him that, but the week before, at the Turners' picnic, Sally said without thinking, 'And this is Thomas Toofat. . . .' Oh, it was utterly withering.

On the night of the dance, no sooner had he come than he said might he go upstairs to wash his hands – he would. My father is always talking about putting in a lavatory downstairs and I shall die if he doesn't – we're the *only* people without one – but I'm sure he never will. Sally and Richard had arrived first and we were standing about in the drawing-room, and I began to wish it wasn't happening, it was such a let-down after the bliss of getting dressed. But when old Toofat came back into the room it got better again because he looked better than usual in his dinner jacket (his own, not his father's). And at least he is old enough to drive a car.

Although Sally and Richard are brother and sister they like dancing together. They are so good, now, from practising, that they despise dancing with other people and that's why Toofat was mostly mine that evening. I had never been to a dance with a man in a dinner jacket. Nine till two, it was, and my latest until then had been eight till twelve.

'Come on children,' said my mother. 'We must start dinner if you don't want to be late.'

She had put candles on the dining-room table, and the little silver dishes for chocolates afterwards, but when I had asked if we could have sherry first she had just laughed. It was utterly mortifying. Toofat's only been at Cambridge for two terms, but he must have thought it positively nursery to be offered no drink at all.

'You look very smashing,' said my father. 'Sally and Lucinda will be the belles of the ball.' He doesn't usually speak in a hearty voice but he seemed to think he ought to then. There's nothing more withering than dinner with grown-ups before a dance, I couldn't *look* at them and I couldn't look at Toofat or Richard either. Sally was wonderful, she talked to my parents about a million things, and Richard talked to my father about sailing and Toofat held forth about being at Cambridge – he's very pompous since he's been there even though he is only a medical student and Sally and I have decided that they don't count as proper undergraduates.

It was easy for the others to behave normally, it wasn't their parents – I'm quite good with Sally's, come to that. But if I talk naturally to my friends in front of my mother and father it doesn't sound natural to my mother and father. 'No one likes an affected girl,' my mother said the other day ('affected' is her *worst* word) – and I hadn't been, I'd only forgotten for a minute that she was there and told someone I'd rather die than read Proust in translation (and I would,

too. I know I got stuck in the first volume, but after I have
been to France I shall be able to do it).

Anyway, dinner was hateful but I had known it would be.
I just sat and felt my skirt round my legs and my hair on
my bare shoulders, and waited for the dance. The truth is I
wouldn't mind going to a dance with a *baboon*. Once the lights
and music and dancing begin it's so fabulous that you don't
need anything extra, though now I rather think I shall when
I fall in love.

They made us go in our car because Toofat's looks fast
though it isn't really, it would fall to pieces if it went over sixty.
And there was a lot of fuss about 'Drive carefully' and 'Don't be
too late', but we got away at last and Sally and Richard
and I started singing in close harmony like we do. If I hadn't
known them so well and if the other man hadn't been Toofat
it would have been like doing something that other people
do, and perhaps as we drove through villages the people who
saw us thought we *were* other people: just a flash of black
and white they'd have seen of the boys, and Sally and me
with our chiffon stoles over our heads and the roses my father
had cut for us pinned to our shoulder straps (because we'd
taken off our coats once we were out of sight). By the time
we got there I was beginning to feel it myself.

A long time ago, when I was twelve, I heard my mother
and Aunt Molly saying how glad they were that they had got
out of going to some dance. At that time I only thought it
was a bit odd but now I think it was the most tragic thing I ever
heard, because if you're so old that you don't even *want* to
dance I can't see that you can want to do anything; and if you

don't want to do anything you might as well be dead. I told Sally about it while we were putting on lipstick (her mother won't let her use it so I agreed not to use mine either until we got there, so that she wouldn't feel silly at dinner. Mine lets me, for parties). We agreed that we would pray to God to let us die before we got as old as that.

Toofat just shuffles from side to side and turns at the corners, but in spite of his flat feet he has a good sense of rhythm – it's not exciting to dance with him but it's not withering – and when we had been twice round the floor he said in his patronising voice, 'You dance very well.' Luckily he's taller than I am. It was easy to look down and hide the fact that I blushed, which of course I did at once. I wasn't blushing because I'd had a compliment. I was doing it because as soon as I have a compliment I think quickly, 'I mustn't blush,' and that makes me. I have always thought that I shall die if I don't grow out of it soon, but later that evening something happened which changed things.

There were plenty of people there who Sally and Richard knew, and Toofat as well, of course, because he gets asked to lots of parties, being a spare man. I knew them too, in a way, but they hadn't got round to thinking of me as someone to meet at a grown-up dance. When we began to mix in with them I could feel sometimes that boys asked me to dance because they felt they had to. They did ask me, though, and I didn't mind much who they were or what they were thinking so long as they danced well, which some of them did. I was in a sort of dream, almost, because it was so beautiful. I danced several times with Toofat, and twice with Richard, and about five times with other people, and then I somehow got attached to the party which the Morgans had brought and somebody introduced me to this extraordinary man.

I didn't hear his name. He was quite old and he came from London. It wasn't so much that he was good-looking, but he had light grey eyes with very black lashes and his nose was thin and crooked so that he looked witty – I thought the minute I saw him that he was probably the most intelligent person there besides me, but because he was so much older I couldn't see how to show him that I was intelligent too. When we began dancing he said: 'Do you like to talk when you dance, or do you prefer to keep it for afterwards?' which was a great relief. Of course I said afterwards. We had a fabulous dance – one of those when my feet can do all kinds of things I didn't know they knew: a floating dance. Afterwards he got me an ice and we sat on a sofa and he said: 'Now. Do you prefer to be flattered, or amused, or disconcerted?'

I *was* disconcerted, of course, but I didn't show it. What I said – and I still think it was very good – was: 'What I really like best is to be enraptured.'

'That's a tall order,' he said. 'You must give me a clue to what sort of thing enraptures you – traveller's tales? Poetry? This season's collections? Visions of eternity?'

'Well,' I said, 'not visions of eternity, because as a matter of fact I'm an atheist' – and I had never told anyone that before, not even Sally, but the way he danced and the way he looked had made me feel very odd.

'A real, thorough-paced atheist?' he asked. 'Not just an agnostic?'

'I *think* I'm a real atheist,' I said.

'That's pretty dashing,' he said, and then I saw that he was laughing at me but to my great surprise I didn't mind at all.

'And I'm a Socialist too,' I told him. 'It's not at all easy to be an atheist and a Socialist where I live, everyone else is fabulously conventional.'

'What are you going to do about it?' he asked. 'Have a one-girl revolution?'

So I told him about going to Oxford when I get back from France, and it turned out that he had been there too, ages ago, about five years I think. He said that the smart thing now was to be a Young Conservative and a Catholic, but he was teasing, and then he told me things I would do at Oxford, quite different from the things Miss Montague told me when she was coaching me for the entrance exam, and much more the kind of things I would like. He said I would go to tea with a different man every day of the week and be a nervous wreck at the end of each term, trying to decide which of them to be seduced by.

Now when he said that about being seduced I was not at all shocked – of course I *shall* be seduced (only that's a silly word) as soon as I want to be – but the word sort of startled me, in connection with myself, and what did I do but start to blush, a really bad one right to the top of my head. I thought it was going to be the most withering moment in my whole life. But instead of pretending not to notice, which is what most people do, this man said in an ordinary voice: 'Do yon find that you blush very easily at nothing? I used to do it too and it was utter misery.'

It was an enormous relief to hear him say that, in such a natural way, and I felt better at once. I told him all about what a terrible mortification my blushing is to me.

'It will stop quite suddenly,' he said. 'Mine did.'

'How old were you when it stopped?' I asked, being naturally very interested.

'I suppose I was about nineteen and a half,' he said.

'Help!' I said. 'That means I've still got nearly three more years of it.' (Which was the silliest thing to say, because I look quite nineteen in that frock and I didn't want him to know I wasn't.)

'But I don't see why you worry,' he said.

'You've just said yourself how much you hated it.'

'Yes, but I was a gawky boy and you're a very pretty girl. If a girl is very pretty she can carry off anything, even blushing. Hasn't anyone ever told you that you look enchanting when your face is pink?'

For about one second I didn't take it in, I truly didn't, but then it dawned on me that I'd just had the most fabulous compliment of my whole life. Of course my parents sometimes say, 'You look pretty in that colour,' and people have told me I dance well, and a boy said to me last year that he liked my hair, and I can see for myself that I haven't got a face like an old boot, but this was different. When I was much younger I used to imagine myself becoming a new person when I grew up – a raving beauty with chestnut-coloured hair – but I realised long ago that people don't change all that much, and since then I've just supposed that I was all right. I never thought that I was *very pretty*. I was so astounded to hear him say it that I didn't blush again, in fact I think I may even have gone pale.

'Did you actually *mean* that?' I asked, and he told me he did. Then he said: 'Bother. There's my next partner adrift by the door – I must go and do my stuff. We must dance again later,' and he looked at me and crinkled his eyes and went off to dance with someone beautiful in a black dress. As a matter of fact I think they were in love with each other because I saw them later dancing with their cheeks touching and their eyes shut, and he didn't ask me again, but after that wonderful conversation I could hardly expect any more.

I ran upstairs to look at myself, and it *did* seem to me that I was very pretty even though my face was quite pink again by then. When I came down I was feeling dreamier than ever and Toofat happened to be at the bottom of the stairs and just put his arm round me and whirled me into the room for a waltz, which he did pretty well. He talked all the time about how, although he despises games, he has decided to take up a sport because he believes that everyone should exercise his will power by doing some things he hates. He wanted to know whether I thought cricket or rugger would be best. I told him cricket because I guess that's easier – he would be very bad at either, you should see his tennis. But wanting to exercise your will power is something I admire, so I decided to stop calling him Toofat, even to myself – and even more so when he went on to say that his favourite occupation is writing poetry. Last term he actually had a poem published in a Cambridge magazine. Really published, in print. I never dreamt I would get to know a poet so soon.

I asked him to tell me his poem but he said it was too complex, it had to be read slowly and that he would explain it to me and give me a signed copy of the magazine. He always talks to me in this patronising way but it seemed almost justified after his revelation. Then I told him a little about my poems and he offered to read them and say if they were any good. A few minutes earlier I would have thought, 'Pompous ass, what a nerve!' but now I felt quite grateful. We began to have a very interesting conversation about poetry. If he didn't talk in such a pompous way which sounds silly coming from someone so fat and pink, he would be a most interesting man, I believe. Also if he didn't sniff so often.

But I must never again be horrible about Toofat – Thomas, I mean – because the next fabulous thing which happened to me that evening happened because of him.

It had got very hot and they had opened the French windows. 'Let's go into the garden for a breath of air,' he said. In the middle of the lawn there was an enormous mulberry tree on which they had strung millions of fairy lights, and the grass where the windows shone on it was brilliant and the night was black with a terrific smell of honeysuckle. It was terribly romantic. We walked past the tree into the shadowy part of the lawn where you couldn't see anything but a few pale dresses floating here and there, and shirt fronts, and the white flowers in the border, just dimly. We were walking along slowly, still talking about poetry and sort of bumping into each other occasionally, when Thomas did an unexpected thing. He put his arm round me.

He didn't say anything special, went on booming about

John Donne as though nothing were happening – but his arm was round me and his hand was on my waist. I wasn't sure whether he had done it absent-mindedly or on purpose, but there it was, his hand on my waist, and it gave me the most extraordinary feelings. First I felt as though I were a girl in a film with a man's arm around her, graceful, with my waist swaying towards him – *me*, doing that! And then I felt as though my bones had gone soft and as though his hand wasn't just touching my dress but was sending rays right down into me – the feeling went right through into my stomach. It was quite different from when someone puts his arm round you for dancing. I almost began to feel sick but it was vital not to show how surprised I was, so I went on saying yes and no to old Toofat in an ordinary voice, while all the time my body was absolutely full of this extraordinary feeling of that hand on my waist, and my mind was full of how this was really happening.

'I suppose we should go back,' he said, when we got to the fence at the end of the lawn, and he squeezed his arm tighter as he turned me round. And then it became even more marvellous. He said in a funny voice, 'You're a very sweet child,' and before I knew what was happening he bent down and kissed me.

His lips were cold and rather sticky from the hock cup he had been drinking. Some people might have been pretty disappointed by that kiss, but luckily for me I read the whole of Thomas Hardy when I was much too young to appreciate it and I have always remembered one thing out of one of his books – I forget which book. A man and a girl are walking

together and he kisses her for the first time and it is disappointing, but Thomas Hardy says that *first kisses always are*. So although in a *way* I had always imagined my first real kiss from a man would be tremendously warm and soft and faint-making, I did actually know that it might not be, and after one second I remembered this. You have to *learn* about lovemaking like you do about dancing – look how I hadn't known about the hand feeling – but I expect some people learn more easily than others and I'm sure I'm going to be one of those.

I stood quite still while Toofat was kissing me – it didn't take long – and I was doing a lot of things all at once: thinking 'This is *me*, being kissed'; remembering Thomas Hardy; noticing the tree with the lights and the green grass outside the windows; listening to the music from the house; smelling the honeysuckle; thinking that I must fix every bit of it in my mind for ever. Then the kiss stopped and we went indoors, still talking as though nothing had happened. And the next time I'm kissed it will be by someone like the man with the crooked nose.

NO LAUGHING MATTER

There had been things not so long ago (or, by Jane's reckoning, *years* ago) that could become strange and tormenting for no reason: a bonfire throbbing and blazing as though for ever, the flames rushing her eyes up into dizzy night; water folding round the pier of a bridge, into which her inability to flow was suddenly an absurd limitation; an afternoon in summer when she had squatted in a tree, wearing a stolen string of amber beads, and something had been going to happen – something so wonderful, so imminent, that its not happening had been unbearable. She had suffered the unbearable there in the tree because of the happening which went on keeping itself to itself through a whole hot afternoon. When she grew older love was like those things. At first she was not always sure whether she was thinking of clothes or a party or men (or a man) because the dazzle of love could be on any of them, not coming out of them but streaming into them from the source in herself out of which the flames and the water and the imminent happening had come. Now, in her first year at the university, it was Stephen who received it.

'Do we think about men too much?' she asked Nora, her head on the book she had brought out to read.

'Yes, I think we do,' said Nora, 'I sometimes try to add together all the hours I spend thinking about men in a week, and it's appalling.'

'We ought to discipline ourselves. Suppose we try not to think about them before lunch?'

'What about getting letters?' asked Nora.

'Oh well, that's different. There's no reason why we shouldn't when they are there to think about. That's common sense. It's day-dreaming that's wrong – I read an article about it once.'

And she turned her cheek onto the book's smooth page (she never expected to do the work she brought out onto the river) and began to think about putting on her pink dress tomorrow afternoon before going to see Stephen: their first meeting that term, which had only just begun. Their first meeting since the decision.

What she had said was nonsense: 'When they are there to think about.' For all twelve weeks of the summer vacation Stephen had been abroad, but to say that he 'was not there' . . . his presence had been felt even by her family. This she had learned when she found her sister's diary:

Jane's too silly for words this summer. She moons about with circles under her eyes for days and then she gets a letter from her love and rushes upstairs to wash her stockings so that she can sing without being told to shut up. I think people in love should

be more dignified and learn to hide it. Ma says it's
her age.

God damn them, God damn them to hell for discussing
me, she had prayed; until she had thought: If they knew what
is really happening they would change their tune. She had
found a pencil and had written, very small, on the wall
behind the reproduction of *The Absinthe Drinker* in her bedroom: 'Christ, that my love were in my arms and I in my
bed again.' Later she had rubbed it out with bread.

She had known Stephen for two terms and had never been
in his bed. They met two or three times a week and always
on Wednesdays. He was living in rooms, not in college, and
every Wednesday she would go to his room for tea and stay
there till they went out together to dine or to meet friends.
The first part – the teatime part – had become a ritual.

She always walked the same way to the square in which he
lived and as she went she looked at everything she passed so
that it would be with her for ever. Soon she could walk with
her eyes shut (when she knew the street was empty) and say,
'Now I am passing the big laburnum tree . . . now the gate-
post which has lost its stone lion . . . now the three new
flagstones in the pavement,' and she would always be right.
In the street leading to his square she passed a junk shop with
a few pewter mugs and cracked soup tureens among the rolls
of linoleum and the bedroom crockery; a fishmonger's at
which she held her breath; a baker's at which she drew it
again. When she rang his bell there was always a wait. The
landlord was fat and had bad legs but he would not allow the

bell to be answered by the young men who lodged with him for fear that he should miss goings-on. He was an official land-lord and could report them to their college authorities if he liked. Wheezing, inquisitive, partly disapproving and partly sly, he would open the door six inches before he opened it wide and her voice would sound false in the hall as she enquired after his legs and his budgerigars. She would go slowly up to the second floor and hesitate before she tapped on Stephen's door, delaying happiness.

She would plan different greetings, sometimes. She would plan to go straight through the door and throw her arms round him saying, 'Oh my love, I have been dying for you.' That was what she felt, but in the end they always met the same way. Stephen's gravest condemnation was *theatrical*. They would kiss each other stiffly, he would take her coat and she would sit on one of the two armchairs, not on the sofa. Soon the landlord would be lumbering up with the tray of tea and until it had come and gone they could not feel alone. A few days apart would have given them enough to talk about while they waited for it and ate it, although enough to talk about was what they usually lacked.

The things she knew about Stephen: he liked rowing, dancing, the *Valse Macabre* and the *Valse Triste*, Americans from the South because of their voices, *The Story of San Michele*, mountain landscapes, old motor cars, tweed rather than worsted. He disliked displays of sentiment, eccentricity, shrill voices, red fingernails, talking about politics or God, his aunts. He distrusted things unfamiliar to him in the way a child distrusts an unfamiliar food: 'I don't like it,' without tasting. He thought himself unintelligent. He had kissed fewer people than she had. Nora found him dull or had said, meaning that, 'He doesn't talk much, does he?'

Jane had answered, 'He's different when we are alone.' She knew he was not but she did not mind. Or rather she believed that although he seemed dull he was not really, it was only that (probably through her fault) they had not yet found the way to communicate easily with words. With her other friends she could talk freely and he, no doubt, could talk as freely with his. Because of the texture of his skin and hair, the flecked green of his eyes, the way his thin hands touched things, he could not be dull. Perhaps he found her dull, too? She hoped he did, for otherwise she might feel superior to him and that she balked at. And if he did it was unimportant because he clearly did not mind it either. He, too, was only waiting for the tea-tray to be taken out.

When it had gone she would move to the sofa, but casually, as though for some other reason; and he for some other reason (to show her a book or put away a gramophone record) would join her on it. This was the time when she had to keep still as though a bird were hopping near her, which made her timid, too. Other men who kissed her admitted what they were doing, often carried the matter further, or tried to, and would talk about it. With Stephen, she felt, it had to happen to them. When, after a breathless pause, it did, she would lie in his arms feeling that this was the highest point of bliss because to dream of any higher point, when he seemed not to, would have been unsuitable. And besides, it was the highest point she had ever reached. More exploratory lovemaking she had already known, had come to expect but could still do without. No one else's gave her so expansive, so complete a pleasure or one so natural, as though his skin under her hands was of the same kind as her own, the taste of his mouth her own taste. She treasured everything about him, the smell of his jacket, the bristles on the back of his neck. She could have been kissed by him for ever, and was for many hours each term. Once, after leaving him, she had said to herself: I love him so much that I would do anything for him, I would *even marry him*. She had told this to Nora and they had both laughed.

'There you are, you see, that shows,' said Nora. 'You couldn't possibly marry a man if it was something you would *even* do for him.'

Jane only laughed again. Yes, of course she knew it was so, but she still felt it, she loved him.

When the end of the summer term had come, the season of balls, they had gone together to that given by his college. Even getting the dress for it had been extraordinary, almost frightening, because it meant twice playing truant and journeying to London for fittings, for which she should have asked permission but did not for fear of refusal. She had never before had a dress made for her in London. She saw it as so beautiful that it gained an almost magical property, and when she went to show it to friends gathered in Nora's room they cried, 'Jane!' And Stephen, tall in evening dress, giving her dinner in a restaurant usually too expensive for them, had looked at her and blushed and said, 'You're looking marvellous.'

After two or three dances a friend of Stephen's had said, 'If you want champagne there's plenty up in my room.' Already a little drunk, they had left the marquee and had gone there expecting to find a party, and the room had been empty. The lights had been out and moonlight was shining through the window showing a glint of bottles and used glasses. Without switching on the light Stephen had poured them wine. 'They must have joined up with another party and moved on to someone else's rooms,' he had said. He had been very quiet for some minutes, sitting beside her on a strange sofa, drinking his champagne. And then he had taken her glass out of her hand and kissed her in a new way; kissed not only her mouth and her eyes but her neck and her breasts. After a little while he had moaned, 'Jane, sweetheart, I can't bear it, we can't just go on and on like this.' The friend's bedroom was next door, curtains drawn, quite dark. 'Come into the other room,' Stephen had said.

Jane had cried. She had wanted to go into the other room, she knew she ought to, not only to prove herself but because this was what she knew, hoped, must happen to her soon. Partly she was breathless at finding kisses not enough for him, partly ashamed at her own naïvety in believing they were. And she was startled – not at the suggestion, but that *he* should make it. Above all she was afraid that she would blunder. She did not know whether he would expect her to undress or not.

To make love with their clothes on seemed to her horrifying (especially in the dress, but that thought she put down quickly). But to stand up in front of him and strip –

would it not seem indecent to someone whose hands had never so much as pushed her skirt above her knee or, until this evening, pulled a dress off her shoulder? Would it not leave them both shy and shivering? And if someone came in, as well they might, two bodies stretched naked on a bed, how would they survive the shock of light, a stranger in the door? And then, she thought, they were not prepared, she might have a baby – but that was finding a reason, her real wish was: Oh why, why doesn't he do something, why doesn't he take off his tie or start unhooking my dress, so that I can be sure?

So she cried and he said, 'Sweetheart, don't, please don't. I didn't mean to frighten you,' and she could have hit him.

Instead she said, 'No, I'm not frightened, truly not. But I didn't know you wanted that.'

'Of course I do,' he said fiercely. 'I haven't thought of anything else for weeks, I can't even work.'

Astonishment, delight, fear. How could she have known that while she had been behaving in the way she supposed him to expect, he had been reading her behaviour as a guide to his own?

'Stephen, I'm sorry,' she said. 'I'm sorry I didn't know. And now it's all so . . . Darling, not here, not tonight. Think how easily they might come back.'

It was true, and he got up and went over to the window where she could see his ruffled hair outlined against the pale light.

'It's the end of term,' he said over his shoulder. 'We won't see each other again for months and months.'

‘Only three,’ she said. ‘Please Stephen. It’s such a thing to decide. Let me get used to it – can’t we leave it till next term? I’ll think about it all the time between and I’ll – I’ll tell you when we meet next term. It’s not a thing I can just *do* like that.’

He came back and sat beside her. ‘I suppose it isn’t,’ he said. ‘I suppose I’m a brute. It’s just that . . . oh well. Look, let’s have a cigarette and then we’ll go and find something to eat.’

She had hoped he would kiss her again, take her back into the warmth and safety of their customary embraces, but she told herself that of course he could not after this. She flinched from ‘something to eat’ as the end of the scene, but what else could he say, what else could they do, now that she had shown herself a fool, a clumsy virgin? She should have melted in his arms – but she did not know how to melt with all those hooks to undo. So she forgave him ‘something to eat.’

They were embarrassed for the rest of the night. They found friends to be with and talked and danced with other people. Unwilling to admit the ball ruined they did the trad-itional thing and danced until breakfast-time, but when that came they were too tired to speak. Slowly he walked her home in the unkind light, gently he kissed her under a red may tree, and they said goodbye.

‘Till next term,’ she said. ‘Darling, till next term . . .’

So the twelve-week separation began and she thought of little else, day after day, night after night, but the decision.

She had made it at once, of course, even before they

parted, but she did not tell him so in her letters. She imagined him in suspense and it excited her. And although she had made the decision, she had to grow accustomed to it.

Only one thing about it did not worry her, and that was what would happen when at last she was there, in Stephen's bed. She had been dismayed by the physical realities of lovemaking when she had first learnt of them, at the age of eleven, but the dismay had soon worn off and since then she had seen every step nearer them as something valuable achieved. She was convinced that it could only be a matter of rapture. It was, in her imagination, the warmth, taste, dizziness of their longest kisses carried on and on to an ill-defined but complete fulfilment. *That* was all right.

The things which worried her were the new relationship of deceit she would be entering with her parents and the world, the completeness of her own committal (though that inspired awe rather than anxiety), the possibility of pregnancy, so alarming that it had to be thought of in one short word, the 'risk', and the practical details. The first three could not be contemplated closely because they were too big: they simply created an atmosphere of menace in which, over and over again, she pondered the fourth – how it was to be done.

Now that she was going to be in her love's bed she could see more clearly than ever how inexperienced he was. She could see him standing in front of a hotel receptionist, holding a pen, hesitating before writing 'Mr and Mrs . . .' His nervousness would be as horrible as her own. To manage it in his rooms, at the mercy of the fat landlord, would be

impossible. How did one know which hotels did not mind? She could borrow Nora's suitcase because Nora's surname, like Stephen's, began with M, but she could not be sure that she would not blush, or that he would not, and if the receptionist said, 'Excuse me, but are you really married?' or even looked it and said there were no rooms free. . . . People were doing it every day in hotels all over the world, it was not a serious difficulty, it could not be. Yet she worried about it all the time when she was not worrying about the chemist.

Nora's friend Helen, who lived in Eastbourne, had been to a doctor. There must have been many other doctors in Eastbourne besides her family's, whereas Jane only had Dr Sims and to ask him for such a thing was unthinkable. She had discovered the name of something but she was not certain how to pronounce it, so that when she asked for it the chemist might not hear and then she would have to say it again, louder. Charing Cross Road was the place to go, because there they put them in the windows and on the counters even, you could point – but on her way back at the end of the vacation she would only just have time enough to make her connection and Charing Cross Road was in the wrong direction.

For twelve weeks these anxieties had buzzed like mosquitoes, teasing at the decision, giving her the circles under her eyes and spoiling her appetite. The more formidable they became, the more certain she was that she would do it in spite of them. The decision was harder than she had expected, involved more than the general principle of the thing which, though frightening, was simple. She was *suffering* for it, and the more she suffered the greater became her exaltation. When the new term began she would go to Stephen (who would still be unsure of her), would go straight through the door into his arms – and at this point she would turn over in bed and hug her pillow, hearing the thump of her heart against the mattress.

So although she talked idly to Nora as they lay together in a punt while golden leaves floated by on the oil-smooth water, the fever inside her was quite out of harmony with the October afternoon.

The next morning she did no work and ate no food. She drank black coffee and walked round the town, sometimes making a violent gesture, banging down a cup or stopping abruptly in the street at a sudden realisation of the slowness of time, at the relentless fact that the minutes and hours ahead of her could not be jumped or telescoped, that she could not run to Stephen through time as she could run through space. She wanted to do everything fast, fast; but instead forced herself to do it slowly. When the time came she changed slowly, brushed her hair slowly, went slowly out to begin the last of the ritual walks to the square, for surely in the future they would be different. 'My love,' she said to herself as she walked along. 'My love, my love, my love.' A white puppy was sitting in front of the junk shop. It came towards her, wriggling its whole body in an effort to wag its tail, and she bent down to greet it. She picked it up and kissed it between its ears. 'Oh puppy,' she said aloud. 'Puppy my love, my dear dear love.'

While she waited for the landlord to open the door she decided that she would, after all, make their greeting today the same as it had always been. She would follow the ritual in every way, so that outwardly the afternoon would be exactly the same as its forerunners, until the moment when the tea-tray was removed. She had suddenly gone beyond any thought of details. She had not been to a chemist, the landlord would be in the house – but then he never did come upstairs after fetching the tray and they could lock the door. She could not wait another day for her love.

Stephen was sunburnt. He took her hands and said, 'It's good to see you,' and she thought his voice shook a little. They had much more to talk about than usual because the vacation lay behind them, full of his travels to be described, and Jane was delighted with herself for the liveliness and naturalness of her interest. He had two new records to play for her, several things to show and a present for her, an Austrian scarf with roses on it. Under their talk the tension screwed tighter and tighter, and she knew that he felt it as well as she did. Her exaltation grew.

When the tray was removed she had reached a state which felt like calm. The evening had grown deep blue outside the window and somewhere down by the river a bugler was practising a call: long, slow, immensely sad. For the rest of my life, she thought, whenever I hear a bugle in the distance, I shall be here. She got up and went directly to the sofa with no excuse. Stephen, as directly, came to join her.

He spoke first.

'Jane,' he said.

'Yes.'

'Listen. I don't think I've thought of anything but us for the whole three months.'

'Me too,' she said softly.

'I've thought and I've thought, and it's frightfully difficult . . . I don't know how to put it, but what I think is . . .'

She had gone cold already. 'Stephen!' she said sharply. 'What is it?'

'Jane, if we do anything silly now – well, we've both got a lot of work to do, and anyway I hadn't realised how awfully difficult it would be, hotels and things, and then there's the risk. I honestly think we ought not to be silly. Jane?'

'Do you mean that we shouldn't sleep together?' She felt astonishment, very dimly at the back of her mind, that her voice should be so steady.

'What I mean is that I think perhaps we shouldn't see each other like this any more, because look what a state we get in.'

'Not see each other at all?' Her voice was not so good this time and the breath she drew sounded almost like a sob.

'Oh, we can *see* each other, there's no need to be theatrical about it. But less. Not alone so much.'

It's not like being hit on the head, she thought. It's like being in the middle of a great black cloud. She stood up. She was almost unconscious, and knew that while it lasted she must get away. She heard herself saying very precisely: 'I hope you don't mind but I think I must go home now.'

'Jane!' he said. 'Don't be miserable, please understand.'

'Let's leave it for now,' she said in the same voice. 'I'm not at all miserable.'

'I'll see you home,' he said. She felt a flicker of hope but it was instantly worse than none because she knew it to be in herself, not in the situation. She had no strength to tell him she would rather go alone.

In absolute silence they went down the stairs, through the square and past the baker's, the fishmonger's and the junk shop. At the corner where the street joined the main road she realised that she would not stay numb much longer. 'Don't come any further,' she said. 'I don't want you to.'

'Well, if you're all right. Look, I'll telephone soon. I'll telephone before the end of the week.'

'Goodbye,' she said.

Crossing the road she looked neither to right nor left. She held onto herself for a minute or two once she was over it, staring straight ahead and walking fast, as though marching, and then she remembered his voice saying 'hotels and things' and she began to sob. She still walked steadily, but the sobs grew louder and more uncontrollable and when she was in the quiet road leading to her college she began to run. She ran the whole length of the road, through the porter's lodge, along the corridor to her room. It had no key. She grabbed her sponge-bag and dressing-gown and ran again, to the bathroom. She filled the bath, her sobs bursting louder under cover of the rushing taps, climbed into it and there she sat, weeping as she had not wept since she was a small child with her mouth square, her eyes screwed shut and tears streaming down and dripping from her chin into the bath water.

Anything silly, she remembered. *Work to do.* 'Oh God!' she cried aloud among her sobs. In jagged thrusts out of the physical discomfort of her weeping came shame for him, shame for herself, incredulous anguish at what life was going to be. *It couldn't be like that.* But it was already. And she had forgotten that crying was like being ill.

She bent her head forward and the tears splashed more directly into the bath water. Opening her eyes a little (already they hardly would) she noticed this and it held her attention for a moment. My tears are mingling with my bath water, she thought, and from some tiny sound spot in all the bruising she watched them do it and was amused. I am amused by my tears, she thought. I'll get over this one day. I'm only nineteen so I'll probably get over it quite soon, and I'll love someone else.

It was as though she had been wrenched in two. Her present self was sobbing in the bath, in the middle of what must surely be destruction; the other, future self was watching. It ought to be a comfort that the watcher was there, capable of one day feeling detached about this, even of thinking it funny – but as that occurred to her Jane crushed her sponge to her mouth to prevent the sobs rising to a scream. 'Oh no!' she begged. 'Promise that won't ever happen. Whatever it may seem to you then, you must remember that *now* it is like this, that it couldn't possibly be more terrible. Please, *please* promise that you will never laugh.'

THE RETURN

'Is bombs from mountain. Not good,' said the man Christos, scraggy at the table over his plate of beans in oil, and wiped his fist across his mouth. 'Bombs,' he said, his ancient-mariner's eye censorious on the two Englishwomen. They sat at the only other table outside the bar or, speaking more accurately, the shack standing as though built of driftwood on the edge of the sea. The women looked in wonder at the bombs, which – or who – were two youths in marigold-printed shirts hanging loose outside their trousers.

These youths were walking slowly past a second time, having come from among olive trees as though with no purpose some five minutes earlier. Across the sea were the mountains of Albania under a rusty haze, so fierce and bare that who could say what violence lurked beyond them. Assassins lived there, it was common knowledge; let a storm blow you to the wrong side of the straits and out of that bony land assassins would spring as though from dragon's teeth to shoot you dead if you so much as sneezed. So were these bombs assassins come across, or Communists or anarchists?

'Scram!' shouted Christos, officious, and the youths kicked pebbles and went away to sulk. Then he put down his knife and leant across the table to confide: 'I not bomb, I gentleman.'

At that the situation suddenly became smaller, the Englishwomen, Jan and Sarah, beginning to understand. Twice, they knew, Christos had been to America, and that was why he was a man of property, owning two boats. Bombs = bums. It was a let-down.

'I take you in *my* boat?' said Christos. 'When you have eaten.'

His boat lay on the water a few yards out, resting on its shadow which might have been carved from a gigantic emerald, while all about the unshadowed water was at this moment aquamarine, great nets of golden ripples for ever sinking through it to lie on the sand beneath. To glide in a boat, leave the bay and land on new beaches only guessed at from sweaty climbs to a nearby headland: this, thought Jan and Sarah, was what they longed for most.

Other boats had been offered and declined. Declined because their owners, in spite of courtesy, had seemed too much moved by a rare chance: these two strange women wandering alone, carrying no burdens, sitting in public with bare arms, idle, foreign, smiling and – surely? – no better than they should be. But the women, either fastidious or not yet much saddened by the years or their circumstances, wanted from fishermen no more than friendly talk and some small knowledge of another kind of life. How pleasant they found the first meetings, and how tedious the subsequent disengagements from which it was sometimes hard to salvage friendliness.

And here was Christos gulping his beans – gulping because how could he chew with only three teeth, two gold, one black? – who must be too old and too ugly to hope for love. This it was, more than his claim to be a gentleman, that decided Jan and Sarah to accept his offer. And besides, he had visited America. Many women he must have seen, on summer days, walking unguarded in bright colours, with bare arms and necks yet still respectable.

They went and ate, returning to the bay in the drugged hour when which was vibration of the sun and which the creaking of cicadas was hard to tell. There, pulled almost to the beach, was Christos's boat and in it Christos and a crew of one. 'Spiro,' Christos said, 'my niece.' Spiro shook hands and dumbly smiled, he knew no word of English, handsome in blue trousers and a white shirt open on a fine chest of hair.

Rocking a little, the boat received them, the outboard motor was started with much ado, Christos shouting orders and Spiro splashing knee-deep in his smart trousers. Then out they moved on to waters deeper but no less still and the two Englishwomen began to dream. 'Boat – *barca*,' said Christos. 'Sea – *thalassa*.' Oh, *thalassa*! At that word the women fell silent, sinking each into her dream of the place they were in, letting her hand trail in the water and seeing it blue even in the palm of a hand.

An hour later, here was a beach to which Christos would put in 'for swim,' he said. A narrow crescent of white sand

cut out of a cliff so tall and smooth that a lizard could not have found a ledge to climb. This great rock wall on one hand and on the other the open sea deep under its blue-black surface; at either end groups of rocks lying where once they had tumbled. To these rocks they went to put on bathing- dresses, the men to one end, the women to the other.

'Our feet,' said Jan in a low voice, 'might be the first that have ever trodden this sand.'

'It is not likely,' said Sarah, 'but that *is* what it feels like.'

Where cliff met water it was bare as elephant hide and blacker, but the water sucking down six inches showed it mossed with yellow-green and lower still, an arm's length under water, it became a feathery garden vanishing down, down, down into another world. Peering downwards, the women floated and swam along this meeting of land and sea, so still and so enticing but troubling because of the thunder of that meeting which lay below the calm. Christos and Spiro, sailor-like, dabbled in the narrow shallows at the beach's edge or searched for shells among the rocks.

They came dripping out of the water together and in a row they sat to dry. 'Good?' asked Christos, and the women answered, 'Very good.' Then Christos turned to Spiro and spoke in Greek, giving orders, and the young man rose, went over to the boat where it lay at the end of a long rope looped round a stone, splashed out to it and came back carrying a picnic. This, wrapped in sacking, was a loaf of bread, a piece of goat's-milk cheese and a bottle – a large bottle – of *ouzo* with four glasses. Oh, are we guests? thought the women, surprised because the manner in which Christos spoke his few words of American had led them to suppose that he, unlike his neighbours, would be hiring, not giving, his boat. Now the situation was a little less simple – but pleasanter, they thought. Because was not the islanders' hospitality renowned, was not the size of the bottle customary? And there were Christos's two gold teeth, now fixed in a crust, guarantees of decorum. So they held out their glasses with a good grace and emptied them with pleasure.

Then Christos, swallowing the last of his crust, turned to Sarah, the younger of the women, and spoke these words:

'You kiss me. She kiss Spiro.'

In the long pause the boat could be heard knocking gently against a rock emerging from the water beside it.

Having hesitated, the women laughed. They rose to their feet laughing and said: 'Come, Christos, it is time to go. We must get dressed.'

Christos answered: 'You no kiss, we no go.'

'Christos!' said Sarah, remembering his boast. 'You gentleman!'

'No, no,' said Christos and he grinned, a distressing sight. 'I not gentleman now, I bomb.'

So there was nothing for it, the women felt, but to walk unhurried to the rocks, to change quite calmly and to re-appear, cancelling with their indifference this unexpected playfulness. Neither looked back till they were hidden, when peeping round a boulder Jan could say, 'At least they haven't followed.' 'But are they getting dressed themselves?' asked Sarah, and the answer was, they were not. Oh what a nuisance, both the women thought as they rubbed sand from feet and put on sandals. And as they folded towels about damp bathing-dresses they both glanced upwards at the cliff but neither said aloud: 'It's true, there is no way to climb out.' Making sure that nothing was left lying, Jan asked carelessly, 'Can you start an outboard motor?' and Sarah answered, 'He wrapped string round something and pulled, but what did he wrap it round?' What, indeed?

They stepped out from among the rocks, dressed, unconcerned, determined. Briskly they went across to where the two men still sat and Jan, picking up the *ouzo* bottle, dumped it on the piece of sacking. 'We will pack up,' she said to Christos, 'while you and Spiro go and change.'

Christos leant back on one elbow. He reached for the bottle, filled his glass and drank. 'You no kiss,' he said, 'and we no go.'

Turning to the younger man the women frowned and shook their heads, pointing to the boat; but he, glancing first at Christos for courage, only smiled, his lips parted, his eyes guilty but eager.

'Now look,' said Jan, 'this is enough foolishness. We will get angry soon. It is time to go.'

To which Christos replied: 'You no kiss, we stay here all night.'

Another silence. New York, the women thought, his age, his teeth, his status; here surely is an old man to whom we can talk sense. But when gravely and hopefully they looked Christos in the eye, there was no such man to be seen. 'Christos!' said Sarah gently in appeal, and hearing her softened voice he gleamed in anticipation, half-rose, caught her hand and pulled her towards him. 'Christos!' she cried out in anger, breaking away, and both men began to laugh.

'We must be more angry,' said Jan quickly and both women raised their heads, knit their brows and in hard voices began to scold. Courteously Christos poured more *ouzo* into Spiro's glass and the men, having drunk, lay back upon the sand and grinned.

'This is too silly,' said Jan to Sarah. 'Come, let us go to the boat.' They turned away and went to where the wavelets laid handkerchief edges of foam upon the sand. They stood by the stone to which the boat was tied and looked at it. At the end of its rope it lay, some ten feet out, rubbing its splintered almost paintless side against a rock, much heavier to look at than they had expected, and a good hour from home. Could they row it? Oh no! While from its stern there hung the recalcitrance of that motor.

The men rose and carrying bottle and glasses they came to stand behind the women, close behind. Christos bent forward so that between the women's heads came a breath of garlic. 'If you no kiss,' he said, 'all day we stay here and all night. I biggest bomb,' and he began to cackle. Emboldened by this sound Spiro shuffled forward and gently put his arm round Jan's middle. She wheeled, she saw his silly grin, and suddenly enraged she caught the glass of *ouzo* from his other hand and flung its contents in his face. He cried out, backed and fell upon his knees, his hand over stinging eyes.

Now! thought the women; oh now what has been done? Will this have changed a joke into a threat? For how still

35

Christos is standing, how silent is the beach. They held their breaths, but a few seconds having hovered, Spiro shook his head, got to his feet, looked first at Christos and began again to laugh. The men spoke briefly in Greek, then turned back to the women. Relish, it seemed, had been added to their game.

Meanwhile the sun had moved. It was hidden now by the cliff's top and the strip of sand looked grey, no longer white. The sea had grown more steely and that cliff, so tall, had moved nearer.

'We can't stand here forever,' exclaimed Sarah, and walked away, Jan beside her, tramping fast through heavy sand, haughty in displeasure; but how to be haughty with conviction when both could see and both the men could see that after thirty yards or less of tramping they would come face to face with unscalable rock? The men came after them, and when they turned, turned too. Bolder with the drink they scuffled nearer, grabbing an arm or laying a hand upon a shoulder, at which each time the women swung round and scolded, stamping their feet and contorting their faces, hoping that where words were meaningless expression would serve.

In this way they crossed the beach several times and neither woman wished to speak to the other, for each had now considered the word 'panic', though only to reject it, and each feared to meet it in the other's eyes. The sand, wet only at times of storm, did not hold the tracks of these absurd pacings but only looked disturbed. The next to land here might wonder what sea monster had come ashore to play.

The careless sea and sky rolled on towards evening, and the cliff gathered a faint chill into its shadow. At last, after what was almost a tussle and a shriller scolding, the men stopped following and withdrew some paces to make themselves comfortable, reclining on the sand, penning the women in at the narrow end of the beach. 'We stay here,' said Christos. 'We stay here all night if you no kiss. I bomb, Spiro bomb.'

It was no longer possible for the women to keep silent together.

'Can he mean it?' muttered Jan. 'Can he really mean it, about all night?'

'How should I know?' said Sarah sharply. 'But look at the bottle, it's more than half empty already, and at this rate . . .'

'What shall we do? I have never been so angry.'

They stared at the sea, they stared at the cliff, they glanced quickly at the waiting men. A minute passed, perhaps, and in that minute they both saw in rapid flashes, hastily suppressed, that things which happen to other people, Sunday-paper things, could happen, might happen, might *be happening* to them. All, they believed, depended on the woman – but they had kept cool, they had been firm, they had neither encouraged nor panicked and here they were with time stretching, absurdity mounting, anger impotent, these unimaginable possibilities beginning to be imagined, and how much longer could they bear it?

Each waited for the other to say it, but Jan it was who at last, and miserably, whispered: 'What do you think would happen if we – well, if we more or less gave in?'

'I have been wondering,' said Sarah.

As though they had understood, the men got up and came towards them. Christos was grinning – his teeth, the monkey jaw, the garlic – but Spiro, noticed Jan, was handsomer when flushed. 'Poor Sarah,' she half-thought, then blushed with horror at the implications of the thought.

Both women felt their mouths gone dry, hands wet and hearts beginning to thump. But 'Christos is yours,' whispered Jan accusingly, and Sarah took one step forward. She paused, she cleared her throat, and then in a shaking voice she said: 'Christos, if we give one kiss – just one – we go?'

Christos nudged Spiro, but he nodded.

'You promise, Christos?' whispered Sarah.

Christos put down the *ouzo* bottle and wiped his hands on the seat of his bathing-pants.

Now, thought the women, the nightmare begins. Now we will have to – will we? – yes we will have to fight, it is too undignified, and it's the struggling, they always say, which ends in . . . but they could not think it quite. They stood with their hands clenched, round eyes fixed on the approaching faces in which narrow eyes gleamed triumphant. The men moved nearer, each came to his woman, reached out his hands and took her by the elbows. The women flinched, screwing up their eyes. The men bent forward and each, softly, touched his lips against his woman's cheek. For less than a second a question hung in the air, hands lingered on arms, and they stepped back. 'Now we go,' said Christos.

As the men walked away to fetch their clothes, Jan caught Sarah's arm. 'No,' she said. 'No, we must not sit down' – for she knew the other's knees as weak as her own. 'We must collect the picnic things and go calmly to the boat.' This they began to do, but hardly had they gathered up the remaining crust and their own two glasses when they heard a shout of laughter. In his trousers and shirt already, Spiro came running out from the rocks, ran stumbling through sand to the boat, wrenched the rope from the anchoring stone, splashed, scrambled aboard and stooped over the engine. He fumbled for an instant, then jerked it into life, took the tiller and the boat began to chug away. He is circling to bring her closer in, they thought, but no – he was heading for home.

At the sound of the motor out came Christos and ran to join the women, now at the water's edge. He dropped his bathing-pants, he dropped the *ouzo* bottle. Raising his hands above his head he shouted in Greek and his incredulity was clear to understand. Spiro waved and shouted back, and whatever his words, to Christos they meant panic. Christos's shouting turned to screaming. He danced on the sand, his face yellow under stubble, in Greek he screamed and sometimes, after all the foreign words he had spoken that afternoon, in English: 'Goddam bastard, come back, come back,' and there was terror in it. Behind him stood the women, quiet. Now they might have been two nieces with an uncle lost to dignity, dismayed at their predicament but furtively amused at his.

After perhaps no more than two minutes Spiro did turn back, laughing like a giant, while the women looked away from Christos's face to spare his panic. He stormed along the beach towards the boat, but Spiro, eyes sparkling, still held the tiller and too much storming would not have been wise. So changing fear and anger into impatience and authority, Christos bundled the women into the boat and grabbed the tiller.

Away they spluttered along the coast on water now Prussian-blue, in three camps: Spiro giggling, Christos muttering and the women breathless and exhausted. But as they went the muttering became less, Spiro's smile, unwillingly, was sometimes returned, and after half an hour the two men drew together, talked and began to laugh. Then 'Boat?' called Christos to the women in the bows, and '*Barca*,' answered the women. 'Sea?' called Christos, '*Thalassa*,' answered the women. And they came again to the bay from which they had set out, the men to tell in triumph of what they had done, the women to keep silent in shame at what they had thought.

A WEEKEND IN THE COUNTRY

They had met two months earlier, in London, where Elizabeth
lived and worked. She had been amused at first to find how
much she enjoyed Richard's company. He did not know the
people she knew or do the things she did, but her childhood
and early youth had been spent in his part of the country, she
had been born into the world from which he came, so that she
understood at once the sort of man he was and felt easy with
him in a secret way which would have been hard to explain to
her usual companions. Elizabeth shared a flat with another
painter, Maggie Brent. When Richard came to London again,
surprisingly soon after their first meeting, he invited her to go
with him to Burlington House for the Royal Academy's
summer show, and she did not tell Maggie. She did not want
to be teased, because she herself was touched. It was unlikely
that Richard would have gone alone. She is a painter, he
had thought, making no distinctions. She will want to go to
the Royal Academy. He had walked round the exhibition
conscientiously, liking best a small painting of his own estuary
– his family's house, he said, was behind a low hill in the left
background – but anxious to learn the point of even the most

'modern' work there. Elizabeth had so far managed to avoid showing him anything of her own except for a few sketches from life, which he had admired. To know so well how he would see things put her in a false position. His incomprehension or dismay at her abstracts would have embarrassed her – for his sake, she felt, though she hardly knew why – so she spared him occasion for such reactions.

He was the son who had stayed at home to run the estate, now that his father was old. One of his brothers was in the navy, the other a doctor with a large practice in the county town. His sister had married a baronet and vanished to Northumberland. In London, among painters and writers and journalists and actors, he seemed improbable; but Elizabeth knew from her own connections that many people like him still existed, unaware that their lives looked strange to anyone. She, of course, was among those to whom they did look strange – only, at the same time, they did not. It was confusing to be so deeply familiar with the strangeness as it came back into her days with Richard, against whom there was no need to rebel, with whom she didn't even wish to argue.

He was attractive to her: a thin dark man, gentle, and rather silent at parties, but no fool. Alone with him, she had discovered that he was an excellent mimic, quick to catch the quality of people, and that he responded (this meant much to her) to sights, sounds and words with a sensitivity not superficial because it was limited. Though he saw beauty only in what was conventionally 'beautiful', he saw it with feeling, and he was not inarticulate. He could not be dismissed tidily as a philistine. To weigh him like this in her private scales made Elizabeth uneasily aware of a fastidiousness bordering on snobbery which she disliked acknowledging in herself.

It had not been easy to keep out of bed with him, but she had done it until now because the relationship's unreality alarmed her. She might not have succeeded if she had not made it a game, on their first evening together, almost to caricature the kind of girl she considered appropriate to him. She had cast Maggie as a duenna-figure – a most unlikely role. That established, and Richard, who stayed with an aunt when he was in London, having no alternative accommodation to offer, it was possible to cut short dangerous goodnight drinks. Richard would clearly have welcomed bed if it had happened, but would not manoeuvre for it too openly unless encouraged; would not, for instance, suggest a hotel until the first steps in an affair had been taken. But Elizabeth's uncharacteristic decorum had created problems instead of dispelling them. What had begun on Richard's side as an attempt at a holiday flutter with someone he had supposed to be conveniently ill-behaved, was becoming serious. Without meaning to, she had driven the hook home, and now he had asked her to spend a weekend in the house behind the hill in the painting.

'Can it be that the landed gent is seriously *épris*?' Maggie had asked.

'Oh, don't be silly. If you live in the wilds the only way you can see people is by having them to stay – it's no more significant than dinner parties are for us.' But it was clear to her that this time it was more than that.

They drove down on Friday afternoon. When they arrived she found that she was seeing the house as Maggie would have seen it, admiring its proportions and the texture of its Georgian brickwork as though she were on a conducted tour of a Stately Home, hearing Maggie's 'Good Lord! How many people do they have to cut the grass?' when she looked out of her bedroom window over the sweep of lawn. There was running water in her room, but she saw the Italian housemaid taking a brass can into Richard's, and in the bathroom there was a Turkey carpet and mahogany casing round the tub. She saved these things up to exaggerate later, with the one glass of sweet dark sherry before dinner, and the talk about dogs and the garden fête to raise funds for the Conservative Party, but at the same time it was all so like her own grandparents' house that even the smells – beeswax in the passages, roses and pot-pourri in the drawing-room, dog-biscuit and gumboots in the back hall – made her feel at home. She smoked less than usual, said the right things in the right way or kept silent, and put on flat shoes the next morning. She was the only person to know that she was out of place, and to give a sign of it, as honesty demanded, became more difficult every minute. She could as easily have picked up the pot-pourri bowl (a Chinese punchbowl, eighteenth century, decorated for the European market – no one had ever bothered to know as much about her grandmother's) and smashed it on the floor.

I am making too much of it, she thought. I am inventing the gulf between us out of some kind of vanity. It is only that they live in the country and I live in London; that they have capital and land, while I have no money but my earnings. Our circumstances are different but we are not creatures of a different kind, there is no *need* to go into disguise.

But still, and largely because this was true, she continued to lie low. It was so comfortable, so pleasant, in many ways so right to be breathing that air again. To have disturbed it would have offended her more than it would have offended Richard and his parents.

On Saturday mild entertainment was provided for her: the doctor brother and his wife over to lunch, a cocktail party in the evening. She had always sulked at the cocktail parties of her years at home, but this, which might have been one of them, began by seeming delightful. There were two pleasures in it: waiting for people to come in on their cues and rejoicing when they did; or catching at the unexpected things, the non-conformist words or attitudes, as though she could carry them back to London and say, 'There, you see! They are not all like you imagine. They are real people.'

Soon she realised that the talk all over the room kept coming back to one subject: the proposed establishment of a 'prison without bars' on a stretch of coast about eight miles away, against which, she gathered, Richard's father was campaigning.

'Isn't it dreadful for them?' said a retired colonel's wife from another part of the county. 'Right on their doorstep like that.'

'But it's not on their land, is it?' asked Elizabeth. 'And surely eight miles is quite a distance? There have been open prisons in other places for years and I can't remember hearing about any trouble. I believe they work wonderfully well, you know.'

'But it will be hideous – just imagine: great barracky buildings and Nissen huts and things, spreading all over one of the few bits of the country that's still really unspoilt. They will have to go right past it – everyone round here will – every time they drive to the station or do a bit of shopping. I think it's outrageous.'

Can they really be so angry, wondered Elizabeth, just because it will spoil a view that hardly anyone sees? Surely they must have a better reason than that. The Vicar made a third in their group, and she turned to him. 'Do you really think it could do any harm to the neighbourhood?' she asked him.

'I suppose nothing might happen for years, but there's always a risk. We have a responsibility to criminals, of course, but it does seem to me that the tendency, nowadays, is to exaggerate the importance of people who have gone wrong – delinquent children and so on – at the expense of the ordinary citizen. After all, we have a responsibility towards him, too. I certainly don't want a lot of convicts straying about the parish. There's no knowing what kind of influence they might have.'

'But I don't think they are allowed . . .' Elizabeth was beginning, when his eye was caught by someone else and he excused himself.

'It's not even as though it would provide work for any of the locals,' she heard a moustached, red-faced man saying. 'They ship in a whole colony of beastly Home Office employees

– the worst sort of minor civil servant – who'll have wretched little glaring red-brick bungalows built for them.'

'I'm sure they don't,' she broke in, roused enough by now to intervene in anyone's talk; then realised suddenly that she had no idea whether they did or didn't, that while his protest was almost certainly ill-informed and emotional, so was hers. 'Anyway,' she went on, 'open prisons have got to be built *somewhere*.'

'And why, may I ask?' said the red-faced man. 'You send a man to prison to punish him, not to give him a holiday in the country.' His light blue eyes stared at her fiercely between sandy lashes and she knew that, even had they not been surrounded by the jostle and noise of the party, she could not have argued with him without becoming angry and rude.

'Well, I think if there have got to be prisons at all, open ones are a good thing,' she said weakly, and he answered, 'But you don't live here, do you?'

Oh dear, she thought, I had better move away and find Richard.

At breakfast the next day his mother said, 'We'll be starting for church at a quarter to eleven, Elizabeth. Will you be coming?'

'I thought we wouldn't, this Sunday,' said Richard, before Elizabeth could decide how far hypocrisy would stretch that day. 'I want to take Elizabeth over to the island and the tide will be wrong after lunch. Can we take a picnic? It will be high water in time for us to get back for dinner.'

'Go quickly and tell Teresa that you won't be here for lunch. I expect she can let you have some cold chicken.' Richard's mother, long accustomed to her family's programmes being dictated by tide and weather, was not put out.

They drove down to a creek some three miles away, where two sailing dinghies and a motor boat were moored. 'I'd forgotten how beautiful it is,' said Elizabeth when she was sitting in the bow of the motor boat, sniffing the smell of mudflats and seaweed. A corner of the scarf over her head was whipping her cheek and although the sensation irritated, so that her hand came up to check the blown silk, it brought back other boats, other creeks, other years so clearly that she left the gesture unfinished: that, and the tock-tock-tock of the motor, and the light popple of water under the bow as they came out of the creek onto the wide reach between the flats and the island. It was ten years since she had been in a boat, and the stretch of coast she had known best had been a little farther south, but it was all as familiar as a dream landscape. When she put her hand on the coiled anchor rope beside her, she found that her fingers had always known the exact degree of roughness and wetness they encountered. She was not sure that Richard, at the tiller, had heard her words, but when she looked back at him he smiled at her pleasure. This was more important to him than showing her his house or his friends. His passion for the place itself, both land and sea, was his rich private territory, the reason why, unlike Elizabeth, he had never felt any need to revolt against the life lived in it.

The island was a bird sanctuary. In the nesting season a guardian stayed on it, camping in a small tarry hut, but otherwise it was uninhabited: a long low strip of dunes

running parallel to the shore to which, at low tide, it appeared to be connected though the mud then exposed was too treacherous to be crossed on foot and the narrow channel of water which remained was deep. Halfway across to it they met the boat in which the garage-keeper's son ferried visitors. He had been over while the tide was still high enough for him to tie up at the jetty, to fetch back the few who had crossed that morning.

'Good,' said Richard. 'We'll have it to ourselves, or almost. I doubt whether we'll be able to get up to the jetty now. We'll anchor a bit farther along and go ashore in the dinghy.'

Clambering from the motor boat into the tiny rowing boat, balancing as she reached up to take the picnic basket and the bundles of towels, Elizabeth began to feel at one with herself for the first time that weekend.

'Come back into the stern,' said Richard, 'then I can get her bow right up onto the beach and you needn't get your feet wet.' But she had already rolled up her jeans and tossed her sandals ashore, looking forward to the silky squeeze of underwater sand between her toes as she helped him pull up the little boat.

'We'll cut straight across to the other side,' he said, and they began to trudge through the dunes.

'I always hated this part of it when we came here as children,' said Elizabeth. 'One's feet sinking so deep, and one's fingers getting cut on the marram grass when one tried to pull oneself up the steep bits. Sand that never has sea over it looks so depressing – ragged old seagulls' feathers sticking out of it, and picnic papers coming unburied.'

'I don't think I've ever hated anything about this place,' said Richard.

'Then you won't ever have enjoyed reaching the other side as much as I used to. It was so lovely – just when one felt one couldn't lug the beastly vacuum bottle, or whatever one had been loaded with, another yard, coming over the top of a dune, and lo and behold it was the last one.'

She did now what she had done in those days: stopped on the crest of the last dune, dropped her burden and stood gazing. There were no other visitors in sight. Immediately below the dunes was a strip more pebble than sand, the chief nesting ground of the terns in which their eggs would lie so perfectly camouflaged that only the guardian's marking sticks betrayed the nests. In the spring the parent birds became miniature dive bombers, swooping with shrill screams at the heads of anyone who intruded, sheering off so nearly too late that Elizabeth remembered putting up her hands to protect her eyes. Beyond the pebbles the beach dipped, then became so flat, sloped so imperceptibly into the sea, that the fall of the tide uncovered yards of it for every few feet on the steeper, shoreward side of the island. Already a great stretch of firm, still-wet sand lay before them, unevenly traced with ripple marks, washed so clean that the occasional shell or strand of weed had the significance of a signature. Here and there shallow pools were draining slowly towards the ebbing waves along courses sometimes lightly channelled, sometimes no more than ribbons of sand more shiny than the rest. To imprint footmarks here was a delight, as though upon new snow.

'Heaven!' said Elizabeth. 'Let's dump the things and walk along to the point to see if there are any seals in today.'

'Do you want to change into bathing things?'

'No, I'll burn.' She remembered that days like this were deceptive, a light breeze cooling the skin so deliciously that the sun's work only made itself felt at the end of the day.

Space, loneliness, high clear sky, flowing air, the turn of a gull's flight and its harsh, lamenting cry – 'I can't bear to walk,' she exclaimed. 'Race you to the sea!' and she was running. To catch a bus, she thought, I must run sometimes for that, but how long is it since I just *ran*? She was astonished at how freely and easily she could do it. When Richard caught her she was hardly out of breath.

'How can you bear to live in a town?' he asked, still holding her hand as they walked on in the wash of the waves.

'When I'm somewhere like this I feel that I can't, but on the other hand I *know* that I couldn't live at home, because I tried it. I don't love London a bit – I don't think I ever shall – but I stopped being miserable when I got there.'

'I could never live anywhere but here. Apart from belonging here, I don't see what could be more beautiful.'

'Oh Richard! Not even Italy or somewhere?'

'Not to me.'

'It's odd that it's beautiful at all. It's a dreary coast when you think of it – flat, just lots of sand blown into heaps here and there, and lots of water that never looks very blue, not even today. I suppose it's the light and the loneliness . . . but other places have those, and more besides. You're very biased.'

'Perhaps I am, but that's how I feel.' He had given her a startled look when she said, 'It's a dreary coast', and now he stared away from her, out to sea.

There were two seals on the barely uncovered sandbank off the tip of the island, but they humped into the water before Elizabeth and Richard were within fifty yards. For some time their inquisitive heads continued to reappear, then they vanished, their absence leaving the sea extraordinarily empty. Small waves curled slowly away along the beach, unfolding so reluctantly that their sound was a part of silence. They were cloudy, full of the tiny particles of life which make good herring grounds, uninviting to swimmers. Gentle though the sea was today, it was not surprising to remember that every few years someone was drowned off the island – even now a gull, bobbing with ducklike placidity a little way out, was being carried past them quite fast on the pull of a current. From where they stood they could see along the coast: a low shoreline, faintly misted even in high summer, its curves slight, the rise of the land minimal. It was a landscape which depended on the sky, and looking at it now, Elizabeth understood why she had never felt at ease among mountains.

'All the sky,' she said, 'from end to end. How awful that in a town one never sees it except in glimpses.'

'During the war I liked the desert because of that,' said Richard. 'It's the only other place I've been in where you could see it all.' Then he pointed. 'See where the mud-flats end, that line of Scotch firs? That's where they want to put that damned prison.'

'Oh dear,' she said, 'what a pity. But I suppose in time it will blend in, and they could hardly have found a place where it would worry fewer people. Any prison is loathsome, but it's such a comfort that they *are* following up the open-prison idea – just think of the other kind! Who was that man yesterday – the one with the moustache? He looked so furious when I said that they have to build these places somewhere, but they do have to, don't they?'

'I suppose so,' said Richard. 'I don't know much about it and to tell the truth I don't want to know. All I *do* know is that I shall stop them building one here if I possibly can.'

She said nothing, standing with her shoulder touching his arm, shocked, yet knowing what he felt as he saw and heard and breathed his private territory. She wished the seals would come back to distract her from her cowardice in not answering him. When they turned to go back along the beach she slipped her arm through his, as though the unquestionable satisfaction of physical closeness could cancel the distance his attitude made. He stooped and kissed her, but lightly. There was a tranquillity between their bodies, and if she had let herself acknowledge it she would have known that it came from expectation, because there was plenty of time.

They chose a wind-scooped hollow, its rim plumed with tall tufts of marram grass, spread their towels and settled down. Sitting or lying, they were sheltered from the breeze, and the sun's weight made them languid. The beer had become warm and although they rinsed their mugs with it before filling them, a few grains of sand still clung.

'Flies inland, sand on the shore: have you ever had a picnic with neither?' asked Elizabeth, brushing at a lettuce leaf with fingers which deposited more grains than they removed.

'On a boat, but then one's mug is always knocked over.'

'So eating out of doors *is* hell?'

'Oh, absolute hell.'

'Then why does one enjoy it so much?'

'Because of what it meant when we were children. Children on a picnic feel like ponies let out to grass after wintering in the stable, so when they are grown up they still keep a bit of the same feeling.'

'Conditioning.'

'If you like to put it that way. I hate jargon.'

'It's funny. You still do all the things we did then, only more so, while I do all the things one wanted to do but couldn't.'

'But I don't think I *did* want to do other things, except the usual nonsense like driving a railway engine or sailing single-handed across the Atlantic.'

'I suppose that's why you are still here.'

'Where else should I be? I like the work – I'm a good farmer though I say it myself – and I like the things I do for fun, and the place will be mine, after all. Do you think I oughtn't to have stayed here?'

'No, of course not. It's just that, to me, the whole thing seems to go with sticking to the same old patterns of thought and behaviour.'

'They wouldn't have become patterns if there wasn't something in them.'

He was sitting with his arms round his knees, looking down at her, smiling a little. Simultaneously she wanted to reach up and run her fingers through his untidy hair, and knew with irritation that he was thinking her too pretty to take her words seriously.

'I really couldn't accept them, you know,' she said earnestly. 'I really couldn't go on voting in the accepted way and going to church in the accepted way and dismissing people in the accepted way because they spoke with a different accent or wore funny clothes, without ever questioning it. My ideas are much more different from yours than you think.'

'But we get on very well, don't we?' he asked, looking distressed.

'Yes, we get on.' The arrogance of adding 'but only because I have kept most of myself shut off from you' was impossible, so instead she reached for the Sunday paper they had brought with them and said, 'Let's see what's new.'

The light dazzled on the page and the headlines seemed irrelevant. After a minute or two she spread the paper under her head, lay back and squinted through her lashes into the profound blue. If she turned her eyes to the left she could see Richard's forearm: warm-looking brown skin, springy dark hairs. She shut her eyes, but could still feel his presence as sharply: his presence, and the very distinct absence of Maggie and his London aunt.

One of her hands lay within a few inches of his ankle. I mustn't let it move, she thought. I mustn't let it creep nearer him. The conscious effort she made to hold it still caused it to hum with invitation, so that when Richard reached out to cover it he was obeying her impulse as much as his own. Only a turn of the wrist was needed now, and their hands would be palm to palm, the current would flow. Elizabeth lay there in a state of suspension, waiting for him to make the gesture.

'Your eyelashes are bleached at the tips,' he said in a voice which sounded muffled, leaning over her. 'I've never noticed that before.'

She opened her eyes wide and was looking into his, very near, his head shutting out the sky. But still his hand did not grip down on hers.

'Elizabeth,' he said.

'Yes?'

'I've been wondering for some time . . . I think you probably know it. . . . Do you think you could bear to come back to live here?'

Oh God, she thought, why must he say it now? She touched his lips, saying, 'Hush Richard. Don't let's talk about it.'

'But we must. I think I love you very much.'

'You don't,' she said softly, staring into his eyes; then sat up and shook back her hair. 'You don't. You really mustn't, because I couldn't come back.'

'How can you be so sure? You love it – I can see you do. And you could go on painting, I'd like you to do that.'

'Richard, I'm terribly sorry, I wish I could – oh darling, you've never even seen my paintings,' she said, half laughing at how absurd that must sound to him, but with her throat beginning to ache. He reached out to put his hand against her cheek and she held it there, leaning her face against it, shutting her eyes. His skin against hers, the empty dunes – the only natural, easy thing would be to lean forward and to rest her head against his shoulder, then let her body slide back onto the tangle of towels and Sunday paper while his came forward to lie against her. It was as though a weight of sleep were bowing her towards him.

'Sweetheart,' he said, 'what does that matter? I don't mind what your paintings are like,' and his other hand closed on her shoulder. With a twist she jerked away from him, scrambling to her feet, the pain of breaking from his touch so sharp that she bit her lip.

'I can't,' she said. 'I can't Richard, I can't. I'd hate it and you'd hate me and I'd be a bitch to you. Oh *why* did you start this, the whole thing is mad.' She turned, plunged down the dune and began to walk away from him along the beach, thinking, Christ! The whole afternoon before the damned tide is high enough for us to leave, where shall I go, what am I to do?

He did not follow or call after her, but quite soon the absurdity of her flight made her stop. She stood listening to the breathing of the sea and to the lamenting gulls, feeling tears running down her cheeks. If not with Richard, with whom could she take her childhood as well as her freedom into bed, and how could she endure the long afternoon with nothing to disguise that loss? Well anyway, she thought, beginning to walk slowly back to where he was still standing, perhaps after this we can do it without lying. But she knew as she approached him that neither of them would find any

peace or pleasure and that it was lucky that she was returning to London the next day by train, alone, because the drive together would be intolerable.

MIDSUMMER NIGHT IN
THE WORKHOUSE

PLEASE DO NOT DETACH LUSTRES FROM THE CHANDELIER. This notice, in purple ink on white card, had not been on the board in the Chinese drawing-room when last Cecilia Mathers looked at it. Unlike many of the admonitions pinned up in Hetherston Hall it carried no explanatory clause such as THE DARK RINGS THEY LEAVE CANNOT BE REMOVED BY POLISHING . . . THOUGH SMALL IN THEMSELVES HAIRS ACCUMULATE AND CAUSE BLOCKAGE. Sometimes Mrs Lucas would address her guests in the third person: MRS LUCAS ASKS GUESTS TO REFRAIN FROM HANGING HATS ON THESE ANTLERS. THEY WERE MR LUCAS'S PRIDE.

'Can he really have liked shooting deer?' Cecilia had asked, shocked, on her first evening. It seemed incongruous in a man whose will had directed a large part of his fortune towards maintaining his house as an asylum for writers and painters.

'People do,' answered Philip Dunn, one of the painters. 'I think he only came to fancy the arts because of the son who was killed. He wrote.' Then, because Cecilia still looked distressed at the idea of owing her three months of repose to a blood-luster, he added: 'Perhaps it was only this one. He may have valued it because it was so *bizarre*.'

Of the six refugees from poverty or domesticity now at Hetherston, Philip was the only one whom Cecilia might have met elsewhere, by choice.

Six was the maximum number of guests, there either by invitation or on application. Cecilia was among them because her publisher thought her pretty and was worried that she could afford to eat only baked beans. He had asked the trust to invite her, a poet veered unexpectedly from Hetherston to Majorca and she was in. But in, so she felt, under false pretences.

For some months she had believed that she did not feel like beginning a second novel, or even a story, because she was so poor and harassed. Given peace and lamb chops for lunch . . . but now that she was given peace and not just lamb chops but roast chicken and asparagus, and summer pudding with cream, she could still find nothing to write. Most guests took full advantage of their time at Hetherston. From ten in the morning till five in the afternoon the silence was broken only by muffled bursts of typing from behind the doors of the big country-house bedrooms now converted into bed-sitting-rooms. Breakfast and dinner were sociable meals – or were supposed to be – but in the hours between no one was disturbed and no one was to speak. Each room had an electric ring and the makings of tea and coffee, while at midday they could help themselves from a buffet in the dining-room watched over gravely by Kerridge, the butler. He was there to see that they had all they wanted, not to enforce the rule of silence, but his presence made it impossible for even the most frivolous to break it. Forks clinked against gold-rimmed Minton china , someone's jaw cracked as he chewed, and back they would drift to continue their work – all except Cecilia. Shut in her room, she would look at her typewriter with loathing and would sometimes almost cry.

It was not for want of trying. She had now been there for five weeks and in that time she had painfully contrived a synopsis of a novel – a structure of cardboard and glue which would clearly fall to pieces if touched. She had also rewritten a story once scrapped and had seen why she had scrapped it. It was hard to sit idle in her pretty room day after day and she would wake each morning after a bad night thinking: No it is impossible, I must go back to London. But so far the food, the comfort, the beauty of the place and the distance between her and unsatisfactory love had prevailed. She wandered about the enormous garden, went for walks, talked to the men on the home farm. Guilt pounced less often out of doors than in. Now it had caught her again in the Chinese drawing-room – the common room – where she had come because it was raining and because it would soon be time for dinner.

Lustres from the chandelier. Who would wish to detach them and how could it be done? The chandelier hung high from the centre of the ceiling. The sofa table stood under it. If you lifted one of the ladder-back Chippendale chairs onto the table and then climbed on that, it would be possible. Someone must have done it or there would have been no notice. Mrs Borrowdale? She weighed over twelve stone.

Laura Preston rarely came into the drawing-room, her work had taken over so she said, damn her gooseberry eyes. Both the painters, Philip and the morose Norman Salviati, were physically capable of it but Philip was terrified of Mrs Lucas and Salviati would not even have noticed the existence of the chandelier. He must once have looked outwards – objects encountered in life were still sometimes recognisable in his canvases – but he never seemed to now. So it must have been Bouncer, thought Cecilia, though it was not easy to picture Charles Opie, smooth and rubbery behind his yellow waist-coat and carnation, balancing on a Chippendale chair to pluck crystal drops.

Opie was there for his celebrity, not because of need. The trust liked a salting of names among its old boys and invited one a year. When Cecilia had arrived, she like the others was met by the handyman in his shirt sleeves driving the guests' station wagon (Mrs Lucas had her Morris Minor). Opie had driven up in his own car, an ancient Alvis. He should have looked foolish, coming up the front drive which no one used. It wandered three-quarters of a mile through the park for the benefit of none but the herd of Ayrshire cows. Grass grew down the middle of it and the remaining gravel was potholed so that the Alvis lurched as it came. But Opie had said smugly that it was the more convenient approach for him, coming as he did from a weekend with Sir Thomas Gregg whose place lay in that direction. He had bustled straight through to the Wing to see Mrs Lucas, instead of waiting like everyone else for the ritual invitation to a glass of sherry before dinner on his first evening.

If Cecilia had been working she would have enjoyed her encounters with their hostess: the first evening and coffee after dinner on Sundays. The trust's London office handled the preliminaries but in the house itself the widow reigned. She had no secretary – it was she herself who wrote the notices. She always greeted guests with the same words: 'Mr Lucas would have been very happy to see you here.' It was devotion to her husband's memory rather than to the arts which made her take so active an interest in the scheme. But by now she had developed a specialist's knowledge of the creative process, as one who sees much of a market garden becomes informed on green-fly and rust. What these people produced she did not care to know, but the symptoms of production were familiar to her and she considered it her duty to ease them if she could.

'So you are a writer,' she had said to Cecilia. 'Are you in the middle of something? No? A pity, that. They sometimes find it hard to start – the change of atmosphere, you know. It takes people different ways. Mr Doherty, the poet, used to find regular exercise very beneficial. He began *two* poems up in the rhododendron wood. But Miss – I forget her name – pretty red-haired girl – plays in verse, I think. She found the best thing was whisky. That was quite awkward. I don't like to ask anyone to leave but in the end I had to. It kept Kerridge up so late – he had to wait until she had gone to sleep and then go in to see that she had not left a lighted cigarette in the bedclothes.'

Philip Dunn's fear of Mrs Lucas began when for the second time she found him asleep in what had once been the rose garden. She had leant on her stick shaking her head. 'It is possible,' she had said, 'that you are one of those who are not suited by soft conditions. There are some like that – like chickens, you know. They need their ration of grit.' Philip's ration of grit at that time would have included nights on park benches. He was angling for the rare privilege of an extension. Mrs Lucas had spoken clinically rather than critically, but he was a persuadable man. He dreaded she might conclude that he should not be there and advise him in so many words to leave. He had rarely been seen in the garden since the incident among the rampaging rose-bushes.

All the flower garden was wild though many plants still won their battle with the weeds. It was beautiful but sad, haunted by its past perfection. Cecilia, knowing that Mr Lucas had been very rich, had expected grandeur. Small amounts of hard-earned money had not taught her how much could be done with large amounts of it. At first, on seeing the neglected flower garden and the small staff, she had been horrified to think that the old woman was compelled by a will to keep up something beyond her means. Now she was beginning to see the estate more clearly. The home farm, for instance, was a model; the kitchen garden was exquisitely run; in winter, they said, the central heating left nothing to be desired and there was the most modern deep-freeze unit in the kitchen to take care of the summer's glut. Only money could nourish so sound a structure, even though there was not enough of it to maintain the elegancies of the past. That the two Italian housemaids got round to each bed-sitting-room no more than twice a week was not an indication of ruin but simply showed that Mrs Lucas knew how best to direct her spending. (And besides, YOU WILL FIND A DUSTER IN THE BOTTOM RIGHT-HAND DRAWER OF YOUR DESK. The widow was not a woman to waste anything, whether the scraps from their meat plates which Kerridge collected in an enamel basin for the dogs, or an artist's occasional need to relax by indulging in some simple manual task.)

Cecilia doubted whether Bouncer, as she and Philip called Charles Opie, ever dusted his desk. His relationship with Mrs Lucas was unlike that of the others. They had friends in common – more than that, the old woman read his books. Most people did, and most critics praised them though they should, Cecilia felt, have known better. He had been described as a budding Somerset Maugham and he had, indeed, learnt several useful tricks from Mr Maugham which he used with assurance to disguise his own vulgarity. The day his advent was announced was the only day since Cecilia's arrival when the five already there had gathered in the Chinese drawing-room with no sign of reluctance or strain. Garrulous, they became, under the influence of resentment. Everyone knew that he had a private income and a perfectly good house in Hampstead; everyone knew that he could work eight hours a day without trouble wherever he was, for this he continually boasted in articles and interviews. Laura Preston knew, moreover, that his reason for accepting the invitation was a base one. His wife had just divorced him because of his affair with a television actress and although the actress loved him he, once free, had become bored with her and wished to escape her recriminations. 'I'd like to know whether Mrs L knows *that*,' said Laura, though none of them had reason to suppose Mrs Lucas interested in her guests' love affairs. 'He's getting his portrait done by Annigoni,' said Philip. 'Monied people have no business here,' said Salviati (but he thought they had no business anywhere, except when he needed to borrow some). Even Mrs Borrowdale, who rarely spoke of anything but the facts of daily life because her opinions were too steady to need discussion, was moved to speak critically. 'I read one of his books,' she said shyly and reluctantly. 'I – er . . . well, it was shoddy stuff.'

Cecilia had been sitting on the balustrade between the terraced lawn and the park when the Alvis came bumping up the drive. 'Do you know where I should park the car?' he had called, taking out his bags. She had gone over to him and he had smiled at her. His eyes, very dark and knowing, were eyes familiar to her – the eyes of a womaniser, saying without any particular intention, 'You delicious thing, what I could do with you!' Her one painless affair had been with a man called Max who had eyes like that, and it had given her a fondness for them. She, too, had smiled, with recognition and pleasure.

At once she saw him notice it. It was as though he had said, 'Aha! Here we go again.' And although she had realised soon afterwards that she liked him no better than she liked his books she could never quite suppress the feeling, now, that they knew each other too well. The way he spoke to her, the lazy passes he made at her – unflattering passes: if they worked they worked, if not no matter – implied that he felt them to be of a kind. They were not, of that she was sure, but her coldness, her withdrawal, remained slightly vitiated by that exchange of looks. She could not quite be free of a man so like Max, when with Max . . . well, never mind.

Alone in the drawing-room at half-past-six, Cecilia had put a record on the player. She was not listening. She was lying on the sofa thinking shall I go, shall I stay, when Charles Opie came in.

'Hullo there,' he said. 'Alone and palely loitering?'

She grimaced a smile but did not answer.

He went straight over to take off the record, assuming that she would prefer him to music.

'I'm dining out this evening,' he said, 'with the Greggs. It's a staggering house. I don't suppose you know it.'

'No, I don't.'

'Why not come? I'll telephone them if you like – I know they wouldn't mind.'

He sat on the arm of the sofa and smiled with crinkled eyes. Opie has charm, see.

'Thanks, but I'd rather stay in. I must work after dinner – it's taken over, as Laura would say.'

He made no answer to that, glancing at her obliquely under thick eyelids in a way that made her certain he saw through her.

'Have you heard the latest?' he asked. 'Orgies in the dorm. Salviati had Rosa in his room last night – the fat Italian girl. Philip saw her come out.'

'There'll be notices on all the men's dressing tables tomorrow,' she said. 'PLEASE DO NOT SLEEP WITH THE MAIDS. IT CAN CAUSE PREGNANCY.'

He laughed and she felt annoyed with herself for making his kind of joke. It happened from time to time and always left her disliking him more.

'There's a new one on the board,' she said, to change the subject.

'The lustres, you mean? Yes, it was Laura.'

'Nonsense, it can't have been.'

'It was, too, she told me. She's got some monstrous child in her novel. Its besotted grandfather hoists it on his shoulders so that it can touch a chandelier and make it tinkle. Old Lolly wasn't detaching them at all – she was trying out the tinkle to find the *mot juste*. There's an artist for you, dear. Kerridge came in and caught her at it.'

'Good God! I wish I had.'

'What are you up to when you spend all day pottering in the kitchen garden? Trying to find the *mot juste* for the smell of organic manure?'

'I must go and wash for dinner,' said Cecilia, getting up. 'Won't you be late for your party?' and she was out of the door before he finished telling her not to be silly, it was not yet seven o'clock.

The kitchen garden was her weakness. It was enclosed within a magnificent serpentine wall stitched with espaliered fruit-trees. Worked by a dedicated man, Philby, it was the only part of the garden still exactly as it had been when the house was itself. Exuberant but controlled, vegetables made patterns against the soft black earth, and there was a smell of fruit, herbs and compost. Two or three times she had diffidently offered Philby her help and he, a thin silent man with kind grey eyes, had accepted it without (she thought) telling Mrs Lucas. While she picked strawberries into a punnet lined with a cabbage leaf, or hoed between rows of lettuces, she felt as though the rest of the garden, beyond the wall, lay about her as beautiful and orderly in its way as Philby's domain still was. She forgot her frustrating struggle to find something to write and began to build up images of an unfamiliar kind of life. Smooth lawns, well-pruned roses, the floor of the Chinese drawing-room not simply clean but glowing again, and smelling of beeswax. The lovely stucco swags over the chimney pieces would not have dust-shadows in their mouldings. They would be flicked daily, as Kerridge had described, by housemaids with fresh feather dusters on long bamboo canes. Instead of queer fish out of water (or leeches, perhaps), there would be men and women who had lived there always – doing what? She would go in from these dreams in the kitchen garden more depressed than before. They gave her the discomfort under the ribs that she associated with the stirring of work, but they had no roots in anything she knew, they could come to nothing. She could feel in advance the falseness there would be in anything which came from her emotion over the beauty of this place. But turning back to what she knew – the tangle of her loves, the ramifications of failure, the gritty details of kipper-smelling stairs, half-pints of milk on windowsills and gas-bills unopened because of fear, she knew that all that was too close, too painful and too boring to do more for her than it had done already.

Supposing, she thought that evening, when she had left Charles and gone up to her room, supposing that I am never able to write anything again? It was frightening. She had long ago resigned herself to being inefficient at living. She could rarely find work that interested her and was bad at work that did not, growing hysterical between disinclination and obsessive scruples. Money ran through her hands as fast when there was more of it as when there was less, but never carelessly, always to an accompaniment of guilt and anxiety. She had never yet been able to love a man prepared to love her – unless he was one who, for some intractable reason, was unable to marry. Perhaps this had been by misfortune to begin with, but now it was made worse by her suspicion that it had become an addiction, that she equated love with pain and could no longer feel it good if it might give pleasure. When she had begun to write – stories at first, and then a novel which found a publisher at once – she had felt like the ugly duckling bending his neck for the first time to his own reflection. Here was her element, this she could do. The horror in wait at Hetherston, nearest in her room but present everywhere, even after dinner when she talked with the others or pub-crawled with Philip, came from the knowledge of how closely her work connected with her own experience and dread that everything of significance in that experience might have been used up.

She would cast back for the scene, the face, the overheard remark that might start to spread ripples, and each time the same things would come up, either done already or weightless as a dead leaf. What had happened to her, ever, except the old sad things, or else the trivia like the nonsense with Max? How do they do it, she wondered, the ones like Bouncer?

'Today I will start a story about a solicitor who has been embezzling his clients' money . . .' and tap, tap, tap they go. Was it because she was a woman? But look at Mrs Borrowdale. In the time left her by marriage that silent woman spent five or six years accumulating her material on aspects of Roman history, then, with her book whole in her mind, would leave Mr Borrowdale to his sister and go away for a few months to write it. A dull woman she would be, if you did not know those admirable books. No, a woman does not have to be like me, thought Cecilia humbly.

Hearing Charles drive away, she went downstairs to wait for dinner. The rain had stopped so she joined Salviati on the lawn outside the dining-room. Had he really slept with Rosa? Yes, he probably had. He was a man who would choose the simplest way available to dispose of a distracting need. Philip shouted from his window to ask the time and soon afterwards came to join them. The other two would not appear until Kerridge sounded the gong.

Evenings at Hetherston went slowly. They all tried – civilised behaviour was a small price to pay for Mrs Lucas's hospitality – but after the first few evenings they had little to talk about. Mrs Borrowdale would fall silent over her embroidery as soon as the talk turned on ideas. Laura would go back to her room. Salviati would attempt an argument with Philip only to have his dogmatism defeated by flippancy. Charles Opie was often out, but when he was in would be little help, irritating the others by talking when they wished to read or listen to records, or infuriating them by not listening when they wished to talk. Cecilia and Philip would sometimes take the station wagon and drive to the nearest town for a visit to the cinema, or to a village pub for darts and beer, but these resources were growing stale. The only unifying factor in the group was a slight regression towards their schooldays on the part of everyone but Mrs Borrowdale as a result of even so mild a degree of institutional living. They joined in a disproportionate interest in what Mrs Lucas said or did, or in childish amusement at some daring infringement of the notices – the time, for example, when Philip *had* hung his grotesque straw hat on Mr Lucas's pride. They also, and as often, split. Laura had become waspish when Cecilia had been invited to after-dinner coffee with their hostess on a Thursday, and Philip's good nature had cracked when Charles had helped himself to a third glass from the modest ration of sherry provided (together with beer and cider with meals – other drink they had to buy for themselves).

This evening they did not go out because Philip had letters to write. It was warm again, sweet-smelling as darkness fell. At about ten, bored by the pluck of Mrs Borrowdale's needle through canvas and by Salviati in a lecturing mood, Cecilia decided to go for a walk. She took the path through the rose garden where reaching branches from the ramblers scattered her with drops and petals, out through the little iron gate and down to the stream which ran through the park. She had not remembered that walking alone in country darkness was so frightening. Her senses became as twitchy as a rabbit's and she jumped when a water rat plopped, a disturbed moorhen scuttered.

When she had made her way almost to the wall of the park she sat on a fallen tree trunk to smoke. The prospect of almost two more months of such evenings, and all for nothing, was oppressive: there was no point in staying much longer. She could find enough money, somehow, to keep her going until she got another job, and if she had really gone dry, this one had better be a solid one. Tomorrow, she decided, she would tell Mrs Lucas that she was leaving.

Her feet were wet and beginning to grow cold. Now that it was really dark it would be easier to get back by striking up through the groups of oaks until she came to the front drive. It was farther away than she expected, and when she had almost fallen because of an invisible dip in the ground, stumbled into a patch of thistles and trodden in a cowpat – an old one, luckily – she began to feel rattled. Gravel under her feet at last, and, I came too far, she was thinking, when there was a loud snort and a shape rose up in front of her. A heifer, as startled as she was, lumbered to its feet and swung its head towards her, there to stand blowing indignantly. Its signal brought other shapes into movement, there was a scrambling of hoofs, more snorting and Cecilia realised that she was surrounded by the herd of young beasts which, unlike the milk cows, were left out all night. Quickly she said to herself, 'I am not afraid of cows,' but her heart was thumping with the shock.

'Good cows,' she said in what she hoped was a soothing voice. 'Don't be silly, it's only me,' and she advanced two steps. The creature ahead of her backed away but the others, with their usual inquisitiveness, began to gather nearer. Their blowing was gentler now but from what she could make out of their shapes their heads were down. Forgetting that in daylight the stance of a curious heifer held no terrors for her, she thought in panic, They're going to charge! She pulled off her scarf and flicked it at them. 'Shoo! Go away!' she shouted, and they jumbled about among themselves but stayed where they were. Oh Lord, thought Cecilia, what an idiotic plight, what am I to do?

She had not heard the Alvis coming along the road beyond the park wall to stop at the gate. Not until Charles put it into gear to come through did she realise that help was at hand. In the time it took him to shut the gate and get back into the car she managed to pull herself together so well that when his headlights caught her she had started walking again, as though making her way calmly through the herd.

'What on earth are you doing?' he said, pulling up beside her.

'Coming back from a walk,' she answered coldly.

'Hop in,' and too quickly she was in the car, safe with the smell of brandy and cigars. Then, unable to keep up the pretence, she began to laugh.

'Thank goodness you turned up,' she said. 'There I was, ambling happily through the night, and suddenly a herd of savage cows sprang out of nowhere.'

'They didn't look very savage to me, but you did. You looked as though you were offering to strangle them with your bare hands.'

'Well, they took me by surprise. How was your party?'

'Not a party, just the family. You ought to have come. The

74

only pretty woman I had to look at all the evening was his great-great-great something or other by Kneller, and she looked prim. And you didn't work after all, so you were just being tiresome. I hope you suffered for it.'

'I did rather. First Mrs B told me how much she saved by using coke instead of anthracite in her boiler, then Salviati began to lecture me on the follies of expressionism. I wish she'd talk about her work and he wouldn't.'

'I wish you'd talk about yourself.'

'The subject bores me,' she said.

He drove past the front door, through the arch into the stable yard where the garage doors stood open. Running the car in beside the station wagon, he switched off ignition and lights together and they were side by side in complete darkness. The engine made ticking sounds as it settled, and, Bother! thought Cecilia, he's going to slide his arm along the back of the seat.

Instead of doing this, Charles reached across her knees and opened the door.

'I want another drink,' he said. 'I've got a bottle of brandy upstairs. I'll bring it down and you must have a nightcap with me to make up for your perversity.'

'I'd love one,' she said, relieved.

When they went out in the evenings, Kerridge put the key of the back door under a brick in the roots of the ivy by the kitchen window. They groped their way in and through to the drawing-room. Cecilia kicked off her sandals and settled on the sofa with her feet under a cushion to warm them. He's not so bad, she thought, while he was upstairs fetching his bottle. Why shouldn't he sell well if that's what people like to read? And a carnation a day is no sillier than Philip's straw hat. But when he came back he began at once on a story about Laura Preston in Greece, refusing to eat dinner because she had seen the lamb on her plate waiting to be slaughtered, lying all day in the sun with its feet tied together, its tongue swollen with thirst. Listening to his mockery of Laura, Cecilia felt fond of her for the first time.

'I'd have done the same,' she said defiantly.

'But you tuck into your mutton chops here,' he said.

'Oh don't be silly, that isn't the point.'

'Have another drink and move your legs over,' he said, coming to sit at the other end of the sofa.

He leant back and looked at her. Again she saw Max's eyes narrowed with automatic charm in Charles's face. They'll still look at women like that when they are eighty, she thought, and then it will be touching – 'What a one he must have been!' – but there'll be years in between when it will be gruesome.

'Why won't you come to bed with me, you silly girl?' he said.

'Oh Charles, for heaven's sake!'

'But why?'

'Because I don't want to.'

'You'd enjoy it, you know.'

'I would not.'

'You would, you know. You ought to let up sometimes on all this doomed love. That's what you go in for, isn't it? Isn't it?'

They have that knack, she thought, seeing a tribe of Charleses and Maxes. They know what kind of woman one is by instinct, on sight, and sometimes it's such a comfort and sometimes, like now, it's infuriating.

'I told you,' she said. 'I get bored talking about myself.'

'Of course you do, if you go on doing such boring things. If you'd just relax and come to bed with me for the fun of it you'd find yourself much better company.'

'Look, Charles,' she said. 'I didn't come to Hetherston to flip in and out of bed with you or anyone else.'

'You don't know yourself, moppet,' he said.

It was far from easy to believe in a fatuousness so complete, but it was not that which made Cecilia lean forward and peer into his face. Do they even share a language? she thought. 'You don't know yourself, moppet.' Different circumstances, of course, but oh Max! He had taken a handful of the hair at the back of her neck (she had worn it longer then) and pulled her head gently back against the arm of the sofa – the cover had been glazed chintz, rather unpleasant – and he had used those very words. And he had been right, too. She had never suspected herself of being able to live six whole months of warmth and easiness, without a bad ending – small but solid to remember even now, and to set against all the rest. Unreal, unimportant, but coming at the right time such a meeting could touch something deeper than its surface implications, might even, had she been another kind of woman, have changed . . .

'Good heavens!' she exclaimed. She still stared at Charles and he stared back.

'Will you?' he said.

'Will I what? Oh – oh no. . . . No, of course I won't.'

'Then what is it?'

'I'm not sure – but thank you very much, thank you a thousand times, dear Charles,' and she began to laugh, while he looked a little hurt at her senseless response. All that raking through the ashes and she had never even remembered Max except to dismiss him. 'You don't know yourself, moppet.' The girl would have to be someone different from her, more like Ellen (and she remembered a girl with whom she had shared rooms for three months two years ago). Oh my God, can this really be going to work?

Disgruntled, Charles got up to refill his glass and she rose too, released by movement and able to say good night and leave him. Going up the shallow curving stairs she ran her hand along the banister and remembered Max's stud-box, dark pigskin, polished with use, and the lotion he used after shaving, too expensive to smell vulgar. Once she had come into a room and had known that he had just left it – the smell had still been there, making her smile. Reaching her room she crossed to the window, opened it and leant out, but she hardly noticed the scent of the roses growing below. Things were hooking onto each other – smells, words, gestures – not yet amounting to a sequence of events but weaving a feeling of Max, a response to that feeling in which at any moment something might happen. I'll call him Louis, she thought, and now I'll be strong-minded and go to bed, because if this is going to work it will still be here in the morning.

She could not sleep. The typewriter squatted on the desk in the darkness across the room. She remembered that Ellen wore a yellow kimono-shaped dressing-gown and saw her sitting cross-legged on an unmade bed in it, watching Max knotting his tie. He was saying: 'Our house was almost burnt down in a bush fire when I was nine. The animals all streamed away from the fire, just like they say, and an old man with a long beard on a white horse came soaring over the gate into our yard.' Ellen had always been Desdemona-like for traveller's tales, that would have been his first attraction for her. What would happen? Cecilia did not know but her ignorance was not worrying. She was feeling the ache under her ribs, becoming more certain every minute that in the mist out of which these details were emerging there was hidden a solid shape. There had been something in the Max nonsense that was not nonsense after all, and if she went slowly, carefully, held onto each detail as it came, she would surely get at what it was.

Putting on her dressing-gown she went to the desk and found a pencil. 'Yellow kimono,' she wrote, then 'bush fire story', 'stud-box' and (to her surprise – it had never happened) 'she finds his wife's nightdress under pillow – doesn't mind – is astonished at this.' Good gracious me, she thought, what are we going to get up to? and went back to sit on her bed feeling restless, not ready to start work but unable to relax.

I want to go home, she thought suddenly. Absurd, with almost two months of leisure left to her. She would sit at that desk tapping away as busily as Laura and Charles, sleep-walking down to lunch, smugly accepting the tribute of

Kerridge's respectful silence, the slippered maids' withdrawal from her room when they found her in it (they were used to leaving it till last, knowing it would often be empty during 'silence time'). She would be a credit to Hetherston before she was done. 'All I needed,' she would report to Mrs Lucas, 'was to have my bottom pinched, so to speak, by a best-selling novelist in a yellow waistcoat.'

She heard footsteps creaking slowly down the passage. They stopped outside her door and she held her breath. There was a gentle tap, repeated a few seconds later when she did not answer. If this is Charles, she thought, I am going to give him such a flea in his ear . . . and she walked quickly to the door and opened it wide. The man who almost fell on top of her was Philip.

'Philip!' she exclaimed. 'What's wrong?'

He took her hand from the knob and shut the door with elaborate care. Then he turned on her a proud smile.

'I'm drunk,' he said. 'I'm *exquisitely* drunk.'

'But weren't you writing letters?'

'I got bored – went out. I *am* so glad you're still up, let's do something gay.'

'But, Philip dear, we can't – everyone's in bed.'

'*You* aren't. What were you doing?' He walked rather stiffly to the foot of her bed and sat down.

She laughed – and suddenly knew that she, too, was feeling drunk. 'I think I was writing a story at last.'

'Isn't that what you do all the time?'

'It hasn't been, not since I've been here,' she said, the shameful secret coming out easily.

'I'm not surprised. How any of us can work in this hellish place beats me. Silence, notices, tact, clinic stuff – and the *evenings*. If I had somewhere to go I'd go, and that's what you should do – we all ought to. Get drunk and hire a motor coach and drive away singing "On Ilkley Moor", like they do on Outings.'

'But it's all right really. It's only us feeling recalcitrant. And don't you think it might be a good idea to go to bed?'

Looking mournful now, he shook his head. Cecilia wished he had not put into words what she had been feeling herself.

'If I go home,' she said, 'it will be hell. I lent my flat to a couple who never go away when you come back – they'll stay and sleep on the floor. And the pipes will leak and the sash-cords will break and bores will ring up and I'll have to buy food – and now I've got this damned *story* to cope with. It really would be awful.'

'You'll go,' said Philip, and her heart lightened to hear him.

'Now,' he said. 'You must think of something mad for us to do before I get unhappy.'

'Why not take your hat down and hang it on the antlers?' she said absently.

'Done it. And a scarf, too.'

'Why not detach a lustre from the chandelier?' – and she could have bitten her tongue, because when he lurched to his feet crying, 'Cecilia! You're a genius!' she saw that he was really drunk and not pretending to be more so than he was. 'Come on,' he said, grabbing her hand. 'That's just what we'll do.'

'Don't be silly,' she said sharply. 'You know quite well I didn't mean it. Now you *must* go to bed or I'll get angry.'

'Oh come on – we'll do it like mice and you can have it as a trophy.' He had already pulled her to the door and got it open so that her protests necessarily became whispered. Snores came from Salviati's room and the uneven tick of the tall clock on the landing was loud.

'Philip honey,' she whispered. 'Stop it – do be sensible,' but a giggle had started to rise in her throat. He hushed her and began to tiptoe heavily towards the stairs, still holding her hand.

'The hosts of Midian,' he croaked. 'Prowl on regardless, girl.'

'Please!' she begged, feeling that she must stop him somehow, although the excitement of night and secrecy, the ridiculous *dare* of the darkened drawing-room across the hall down below, had begun to touch her as well as him.

As they went down the stairs her fluster increased. Dismay at what he might get up to, shame at the childishness of having come this far, were mixed with an absurd elation: she had her story! She could write it here, there or anywhere, but what had they to do with her, these well-meaning people who left houses for her and made no terms? Of course she would leave Hetherston – at once, while the story was still brewing up. Why suffer another evening when the comfort, the beauty and Philby's kitchen garden would have become meaningless, having no gap to fill? She must be on her own and back in real life, to get on with it.

Philip switched on only one of the wall-lights in the

Chinese drawing-room. It was large and shadowy, a lovely room from another life, the loveliest thing in it the great glass shower in its centre. Cecilia, who owned few objects, was scrupulously respectful of other people's – but she found herself looking at this one as though it had no owner, were a cairn from which you picked a stone to prove that you had been there. Philip, who had gone quiet, lifted a chair but she stopped him. She found a copy of the *Times Literary Supplement* to spread on the shining top of the sofa table, then let him stand the chair on that. He was beginning to look glazed and did it clumsily. He was no longer, she saw, to be trusted as a climber.

'Shall I?' she asked, still whispering, and he nodded.

The table complained as she climbed onto it, but it was steady. Very carefully, distributing her weight evenly, she mounted the chair, stood up and reached into the centre of the chandelier. From one of its inner circles she detached two faceted lustres, handed one down to Philip and slipped the other into her dressing-gown pocket.

Philip helped her down and stood swaying slightly while she put everything back where it should be. She had a moment's fear that she would not be able to get him up the stairs, but he pulled himself together and made it. Having seen him to his room she returned to her own and got into bed. For a little while she lay on her back staring into darkness, wondering what on earth had made her do such a silly thing – such an outrageous thing, really. Then, feeling very happy, she turned on her side and went to sleep.

FOR RAIN IT HATH
A FRIENDLY SOUND

Dry earth under a shower of rain: a few words on the telephone had made Kate Beeston feel like that. She put the receiver down gently and went to sit on a corner of the kitchen table, her hands heavy on her knees as she stared out of the window. When Robert, her husband, went past pushing a wheelbarrow, her eyes followed him and she knew that he was engaged on the first part of his plan for the weekend which, as usual, he had written out in a special notebook on Friday evening. Her expression became neither amused nor irritated. She looked like a woman dreaming over a book, as though behind her square freckled face there moved some beloved character from pages just put aside.

The name had stabbed – 'It's David Field here' – so that Kate had reached for something to lean on, but then an odd contentment had come down on her and it had been an effort to understand what he was saying. She had wanted only to listen to the sound of his voice. He had called to say that he knew the Italian girl employed by the Masons, whom he was treating for bronchitis, was unhappy with them.

If Kate still needed a maid, now was the time to act. It must have been four months ago, the last time she saw him, that she had said something in his hearing about looking for a maid to live in.

'If I were twenty-five,' she thought, 'I would be up in my room recovering, sure that the call was an excuse to speak to me again. But I am thirty-seven and David is a kind man with a good memory, worried about that girl and pleased to think that in helping her he may also help a woman he likes, with whom he once spent a week.'

The Fields lived ten miles away, in the county town, and David was not the Beestons' doctor. The paper-mill of which Robert Beeston was a director was on the outskirts of the town, but Kate and Robert had always known more people to the north of the county: one of those with a mysterious division across it, almost like a watershed, so that people living only a few miles apart would refer to each other as being 'north' or 'south' as though that fully explained the lack of intimacy between them. Because of this, Kate had met David's wife no more than a score of times in twelve years.

On their few meetings during the last three of those years, Kate had watched Penelope Field across rooms, moved nearer to overhear what she spoke about. She was an odd-looking woman with a crooked mouth, well dressed, reserved, sometimes abrupt in her manner. Kate knew people who found her rude and others who said she was boring, but she herself saw Penelope in an aura of privilege and certainty and believed that to her close friends she must reveal extraordinary qualities. She knew she was imagining it when the other woman's dark eyes seemed to fix her with an attention equal to her own and that Penelope's remote manner when they spoke was her usual one, no indication that she had learnt about Kate and David.

Three years ago Robert Beeston had gone to Canada for his firm. He had gone reluctantly, disliking unknown places, but Kate had much looked forward to his journey. She had hoped that he might enjoy it and that this would make him more receptive to ideas of travel, for whenever she suggested the holidays abroad for which she longed, he countered with a walking tour in Wales. He could only imagine relaxation in walking, and then only in places hallowed by discovery during his boyhood. Year after year – on the Coué principle, she supposed – he would begin discussion of such a holiday as though she shared his enthusiasm, and year after year he would grow angry at what he considered her perversity in not sharing it. 'Does he really forget?' she would wonder. 'Or has he never *listened*?'

Anyway, she had felt, whether Canada worked on him or not, his absence would rest her, for they had been having some bad months. Something had rubbed a hole in Robert's extraordinary talent for not noticing the disagreeable in the familiar, he had begun to see that she was unhappy and had been in a constant temper about it. Unhappy himself, Kate had supposed, being fair: but he was so deft at turning an uncomfortable emotion into one he could handle that it was hard for her to keep sight of his mood's origin. She had done her best to avoid quarrels. He was jealous of anything they did not have in common: her work in London before their marriage; her friends from that time, none of them business-men or landowners; her uncertain but adventurous taste in pictures, decoration, clothes. Trying to reassure him, she had given away a pair of orange slacks and often wore a light-blue dress he had chosen for her, although she detested light blue with red hair; she had long stopped talking politics with him and would find a reason for drifting out of the conversation when he talked them with other people; she rarely tried to discuss the books she enjoyed; she no longer invited her old friends to stay. From good nature rather than conviction she had always tended to assume that other people were more likely to be right than she was, so that over the years it had not been hard to send many of her inclinations underground rather than contend with him as he settled in ways she had not expected. She could not see that she was grudging this more obviously than before. Their joint life was full enough with children, house, garden, the pleasures still shared such as their feeling for animals and the country; Kate could forget her dissatisfaction for weeks on end, for as long as Robert remained unaware of it. But the accumulation of her silences must have been more eloquent than the open disagreement of their early days, and belatedly he had started to nag. 'I can't see what right you've got to despise so and so,' he would say, when she had in fact succeeded in persuading herself that the man was pleasant company; or, 'Of course, it would be too lowbrow for *you*,' of some book she might well have enjoyed reading. Maddeningly, he was almost always wrong in detail, but his uneasiness and resentment, unhappily she knew it, were based on the truth.

So she had looked forward to his three weeks in Canada. The children were both at school, she would go to London. She was becoming absurdly rooted, finding it increasingly hard to go away even for a night: what to do with the dogs? who would feed the children's birds? when, if not then, would she get the delphiniums staked? None of these problems was real. The Beestons employed a part-time gardener and could call on two women in the village for help in the house, but still Kate would find herself fatigued and discouraged at the effort of departure as though some faculty in her were becoming crippled. This time, too, the familiar impotence crept up, almost deciding her to stay. But just before he left she and Robert had skidded into an open quarrel which left her thinking, 'I'm mad. I'm letting inertia trap me into lunacy. It's only a matter of making a few telephone calls, buying a railway ticket, and of course I can go.' When she was a child her nanny used to scold her for coughing. 'Now then, dear, stop it,' she used to say. 'It's all on your mind.' And sure enough, once she began to act Kate found that her obligations, even the seriousness of Robert's disapproval ('But what on earth will you *do* in London for so long?'), were mostly 'on her mind'.

She caught her train, she stayed not with her sister, as Robert expected, but in a hotel, and she spent the best part of three sunny days neither shopping nor visiting exhibitions but lying on the grass in a park. 'Why go to *London* to lie on *grass*?' Robert would have said if he had known, and how would she have explained it? 'We don't have Chinese geese at home,' she might have said, watching them in dignified procession by the waterside. 'We don't have ragged little boys gunning for each other from behind chestnut trees, but being so patient with the baby in the pram which they have to tag along with them. We don't have old men spreading newspapers on benches and sitting on them to scold greedy pigeons who chase their wives away from breadcrumbs.' Silly answers, she thought, were all she could have given Robert as she lay feeling herself flow out into every corner of her body, looking out of her eyes at things as though they were new.

On the fourth day, restored, she went gaily to a cocktail party and David Field was there, one of a few more or less familiar county faces. The Londoners made her a little shy so she crossed the room to stand beside him. Penelope was in Italy. 'I couldn't get away,' he said, 'but Pen can't endure a summer without going abroad.' He seemed to take it for granted that if someone wanted to do something he should, if possible, do it. If Kate had suggested a holiday without Robert, he would have doubted her sanity. He himself would always refuse to go to a party without her, even when they both knew that he would enjoy it and she would not: his forehead would flush with indignation and he would say, 'You want to spoil my evening.' Kate remembered hearing people comment on the Fields' independence of each other. 'Do you often do things separately?' she asked, not wholly disguising envy, and as they talked she understood that his attitude did not spring from indifference. It was simply that he loved his wife with generosity.

Quite soon she became frightened. It seemed to her that she *knew his face too well*. It was a familiarity unconnected with their chance meetings at home, coming ('I must be drunk,' she thought) from the future. She listened attentively enough – with unusual attention, even, for she had not known that he was so amusing, so easy – but while she listened she was also watching. Half scared, half elated, she was following the line of his eyebrows as though she had often – would often – run a finger along them; was recognising the high, rather starved cheekbones, the way his mouth pulled down at the corners when he smiled. It was too improbable for serious alarm, but 'That's a face I'm going to love,' she knew, as though dreaming.

'You'll have dinner with me,' said David, and when they were settled in a restaurant they really started to talk. It was a return to her own language after years of speaking another which, however well she knew it, had always been more of an effort than she realised. They talked about their friends and their children: ordinary things, but they could tell the truth about them, and something inside Kate relaxed, spread, glowed. It would be easy to go on talking and laughing like this for all her life. And as the evening went on she saw that this almost unknown man who showed so clearly that his life was full of satisfactions, was nevertheless prepared to look at her with pleasure and a startling intimacy. 'Is he rather a devil?' she wondered, more interested than dismayed by the unexpectedness of it.

David, in London for a series of meetings, had been lent a friend's flat for a week. She went back with him for a last drink and when, halfway up the stairs, he turned in the middle of a sentence to kiss her cheek, it was almost too natural to notice.

Half an hour later she stubbed out a cigarette and said regretfully, 'Oh well, I suppose I must get back to my hotel.' He picked up her coat, hesitated, then said: 'You know, it would be much *much* nicer if you would stay here with me.' Kate had begun to say, 'Dear David, don't be ridiculous,' when she stopped, knowing: 'But that's the exact truth. It would be much *much* nicer.' So she took the coat and put it slowly back on the chair from which he had lifted it. He caught her by the shoulders and they both laughed. She stayed with him all that week.

Not for one moment did Kate suppose that it would change their ways of living. David was too practised to warn her in so many words, 'I love my wife,' but there it was. He did. He wanted Kate with him, she soon discovered, because he hated being alone, because he liked her and found her attractive, because he was a man rational almost to ruthlessness who could see no good in being cold when he might be warm, lonely when he might be enjoying himself. Being ready to allow others their own natures, he did not hesitate to indulge his own. Kate herself was like that up to a point and, sensing it, he gave her credit (conveniently) for being more like it than she was. He assumed that she was as much in control of what she was doing as he was.

For this she knew that she might blame him in the future, but there was so much else for which she could feel only gratitude and love. Some years earlier she had become a light sleeper and had won a bed to herself. She had always treasured it. When Robert returned to his own she would have to resist a longing to get up, smooth the sheets, plump the pillows, remove all signs of its dishevelment and make it again her private territory. And now, a little awkwardly, almost like a girl, she was exploring an intimacy which only seemed delightful. She would wake in the night and move gently nearer David so that she could feel his back against her own; she would hesitate to pull her arm from under his neck when it became painful; she could even watch a man cleaning his teeth with pleasure and was disappointed if he did not come to sit on the edge of the bath when she was in it. And she marvelled all the time that any two people could so understand each other and that someone could be, in any degree of love, so like her own conception of it as David was. For those few days he gave her, in a small way, she knew, but truly, what he gave his wife: appreciation for what she was, his pleasure in her as an individual rather than as a reflection of his wishes, the warmth of a man accustomed to loving rather than possessing.

Explanations were rarely necessary between them. 'Do you ever feel guilty about this sort of thing?' she asked him once, knowing without being told that he had done it before. 'No,' he said. 'Why should one's obsessions dominate every corner of one's life? This is real too,' and that was all she needed to be told about his relations with Penelope. How could this delight and ease, however real, compete with obsession? 'You and I would probably have got married,' he said later, 'if we had met long ago': words with which she had lived ever since, both steadied by their coldness and warmed by their comfort.

When she got home she remained happy for two days. The week just past overflowed into those days, David was in her bones, she could not feel that he was gone. Robert was not yet back, there was nothing to disturb her reliving of that week. But the pain had begun before her solitude was over.

She knew very well that David would neither write nor telephone, but her body, she found, was charged with complete incredulity, responding instantly and violently to letters on the mat, the ring of the bell. This physical impact of loss horrified her. 'I must control myself, I must control myself,' she muttered aloud, on the third evening alone, but still her body paced backwards and forwards across her bedroom until she cried out, 'But what am I going to do?' Her aching throat made her hope: 'Perhaps crying will make it better?' But the tears took control, she made noises like an animal, the weeping hurt her whole body, scorched her eyes, drove her down to the kitchen in desperation to make herself tea as though she were a victim of shock. And it was worse when the tears were over. 'Have a good cry,' people said! The physical humiliation ebbed, and there was the grey weight of loss, untouched, undiminished.

Her sense of loss was so terrible that it eclipsed her dread of Robert's return. When a telegram came, announcing the time of his arrival, she stared at it expecting panic but found it unimportant. It was only a matter of thinking up a way to explain her haggard looks and to postpone his lovemaking.

She pleaded illness: a bilious attack which had turned out worse than she had expected and had left her low. He found her nerviness extraordinary, quite unlike her, and made her go to the doctor. Forced, gradually, to pull herself together, she drank her tonic and thought, 'Why not? Why not treat grief as an illness? There's nothing else I can do about it.'

It was a question, she began to see, of dealing with symptoms as they occurred and waiting for time to pass. To be busy, to be brutal with herself: those were the only specifics. When the pain became unbearable she would allow herself a small dose of self-indulgence: as she pruned roses or polished furniture she would kill Penelope in an air crash, bundle Robert into love with a widow who had children of her own and would not want Kate's, and then she would begin to dream times and places with David. But having shared so little with him, her resources for these dreams were limited, and her sense of their absurdity was strong. 'Fool!' she would have to conclude. 'He does not love you, it is not even as though he were remembering you,' and to this abrasive knowledge she would cling. A loss existing only 'on her mind' must surely stop torturing after a while.

Kate thought, in those first months, how mistaken were people who spoke of children as though they were everything; who would comfort themselves for some woman's loss of her husband with the words 'Luckily she has the children.' They might as well have said, 'Luckily she has her hands.' Without them God help her, certainly; but children were children and a man was a man, there could be no substitution. James and Muffie came home for the holidays as much a part of her as ever, their non-existence unimaginable. 'Of course I love them,' she would have snapped at anyone who had asked, angry at the pointlessness of the question, but the things about them by which she was ridden at that time were their demands, their failings, the anxieties and chores they carried in their wake. Guiltily she recognised that she had become almost unable to take pleasure in them; and worse, she would catch herself looking at them with detachment, thinking, 'And after all, why should I? James has no imagination, he will grow into a dull man, and Muffie in her present exhibitionist phase is even displeasing.' She felt dry and ugly, knowing herself now a woman married to a man who often bored her, loving children who could no longer enchant her.

Robert agreed to their building out a playroom for the children, and this Kate insisted on planning and decorating herself. She worked hard. After a while she no longer had to fight against the pain's magnetism in every unoccupied moment and even began to shy away from it. When it was touched off by a word or thought she would surprise herself by thinking, 'Oh God, no! I can't stand any more of that,' and turning to something else. A whole morning would go by and would realise, 'I haven't thought of David since I got up.' And then a whole day, and she knew that she was mastering it. But she was haunted by the knowledge that sooner or later she would come into a room and see him talking to her hostess, or run into him in the street when she was shopping in the town.

That was how it happened at last, after nearly six months of carefulness and luck. She had warning. She had taken the children to Woolworths to do their Christmas shopping and there, studying a tray of clockwork tanks, she saw his sons. David himself was not in the shop as far as she could see, and she decided that she was probably safe. This was a mother's job, they would be with Penelope. But still it was not pure shock when she came out through the swing doors to find him sitting in his car, waiting for his family.

He got out and came to take her hand. 'How nice to see you,' he said. 'Did you by any chance notice two of my young in that inferno?' She had told herself from time to time during her 'cure' that she had built up an imaginary David and that when she met him again she would find him diminished, but no. This, she knew at once, was the face and the voice she loved.

'They're buying tanks,' she answered, and already because he was there she was relaxing, spreading, glowing as she had done before. For some minutes they stood on the pavement, talking of this and that. She followed him in using the tone of old friends – closer friends than they would have been without their week together, but with no recognition of that week – and it was not only easy but pleasant. How could she have dreaded something that was all she longed for?

When David's sons came out of the shop he was angry with them because, having been given half an hour for their shopping, they had kept him waiting. 'Into the boot with all that junk,' he said severely, 'and be quick about it.' But as he opened the door for them and the youngest boy bent forward to stow his parcels, he ran his hand over the child's head. 'I'm bad at discipline,' he said as the boys jostled their way into the car. 'It's the backs of their necks that undo me. When I want to be stern I always avoid looking at them from the back.'

That he should have felt and said something so unexpectedly feminine seemed to Kate like a piece of amber to be picked up on a pebbly beach. Several times, as she was driving home, she smiled at it; and that evening, when James came to show himself well bathed, she said: 'Yes, you're my clean and handsome one,' and kissed the back of his neck. Later she had to struggle against tears and could not bring herself to go into the bedroom until she was sure that Robert was asleep, but the revival of loss was accompanied by a revival of a sense of David's existence outside her mind, and this – it was strange, she had not expected it – was warming.

Before a year had passed she had almost stopped thinking of him, but each of their few meetings she could remember down to the smallest detail of expression. In three years there had been two more encounters in the town, one occasion when the Fields' car had been parked beside the Beestons' at a race meeting and she and David had spent twenty minutes together in the group by the water-jump, two cocktail parties and the dinner party, four months ago, at which he had heard her talking about maids. Penelope was always there as well. At one of the cocktail parties David had smiled at Kate with particular intimacy when she made a joke that no one else noticed, and at the race meeting he had referred quite naturally to an exhibition they had visited during their week; but what she brought back from the meetings was chiefly confirmation of his tenderness towards his wife. 'That woman wears the trousers,' Robert remarked on one occasion, and Kate had agreed, getting some satisfaction from spitefulness, but what she really felt was: 'That man knows how to love.' To see it strengthened her 'cure' – and at the same time established that what had happened could not be thought away. She could stop herself – had stopped herself – from loving, but David had not changed from being a man she could love.

'I was not an hysterical fool,' she said to herself now, so long after it had happened, sitting on the kitchen table after his telephone call. 'I wasn't making him up because I needed to fall in love; he *is* the nicest man.' That he should have thought of her, even remembered her casual words after such a long interval, made her see him as a paragon of kindness. 'Of course he must really have remembered me quite often,' she thought. 'That week happened to him, too.'

Robert shouted to her from the garden. She went out and found him on his way down to the boggy meadow which adjoined their orchard, some of which they wanted to enclose as additional vegetable garden.

'If we dug a deep ditch across the bottom,' he said, prodding the ground, 'and then ran two drains down there and there, it would be dry enough in no time.'

They would have to get extra labour for the ditches, she said, it would be too much for him and the gardener, and he agreed. They stood together amicably in the sun, wondering whether they could have a primula garden along the deep ditch when it was dug, or whether primulas needed more shade. The grass was young and succulent, buttercups were beginning to come out, and from the hedge round the orchard the peppery smell of hawthorn came drifting. As they walked back towards the house they both paused to look up through flowering branches at the sky, so intensely blue beyond the snow of blossom.

'*Can't* we go to Spain this year?' she said.

'I don't care what you say,' he answered, 'it would be lunacy to take the children. That revolting food would finish me at once, so what it would do to them, God knows. It beats me how you can be so unrealistic.'

'But they're not babies any more, and other people do it all the time. Anyway, what's so dreadful about a tummy upset? We could stock up with sulpha medicines and if any of us did get ill it would soon be over.'

She knew, though, that he would soon come up with his walking tour – not in Wales, perhaps, this time: Scotland or the Lake District, as a concession, or even Brittany. 'Poor old boy,' she thought, 'it would be cruel to drag him off somewhere he hated, he does work so hard all the year' – but only twice in all the years of their marriage had she done it, while he had won again and again.

Back in the kitchen, breading the chops for lunch, she watched him through the window. He had noticed that the clothes-line was beginning to sag and he was straightening the pole which held it. It always pleased Kate to watch him working with his hands, absorbed and grave, like James playing with his trains, but handsome though he was – 'And he is still very good-looking,' she thought with surprise – it astonished her now to remember that she had once found him physically disturbing. While as for his mind . . . 'He is extraordinary,' she thought. 'Fifteen years, and he still can't even accept that we don't always like the same things. Can he really be as impermeable as he seems, or is he a wicked old bully?' She shook her head as she worked, but although she did not know it she was smiling slightly.

After lunch she went back into the orchard alone. She pulled down a branch of an apple tree to look at the thickening green thalami, some with a few petals still adhering (one doesn't wander in one's own garden for no reason, she was estimating the year's crop, they would think). She wanted to be undisturbed for a few minutes so that she could remember David's voice on the telephone. She stood quite still, relaxed, not at all dry or ugly. 'Well, anyway,' she thought, 'there *is* a man in the world I could love.' She leant her cheek sideways so that it was brushed by leaves. 'After I'm dead,' she thought, 'the apples will go on bearing and the hawthorn will go on flowering, year after year,' and she felt so calm that it was almost happiness. Later that day she wrote to Thomas Cook's for details about travel in Spain.

AN AFTERNOON OFF

Roger Paul, who in his good tweed suit looked more like an intelligent soldier than a publisher, began to walk slowly down the street. He saw a stationer's noticeboard on which a muscular and broad-minded young man offered to massage either ladies or gentlemen, followed by six Italian shoes of different colours. Then a string of onions hung above a wicker basket of red peppers, two copper moulds in the shape of fish crowned an arrangement of wooden pepper-mills, an old man with one arm played a small concertina strapped to his chest and a Negro or half-Negro prostitute with blonde hair wore a sugar-pink duffel coat. Thursday afternoon in Soho, bright and clear, each object suddenly startling to Roger Paul. Even a torn poster saying And Woman Was Created, half covering another poster saying Around The World in.

He had finished his last lunch with Herr Becker, whom he had put into a taxi and dispatched to his hotel to pack. Naomi would take him to the airport. She and Roger, who was recently divorced, had fewer social obligations than the others and undertook most of such duties. The week of bear-leading through press conferences and television studios was over and at lunch Becker had talked again, and talked well, about his life among the Berbers while Roger had watched his face and thought *beastly bloody kraut*. The German, once a prisoner of war in the Western Desert, had made an unlikely escape and had survived in a way which would have been impossible if he had not been brave, intelligent and likeable, at least to Berbers; which, indeed, the book he had written suggested that he was. But he had a steep narrow forehead and small light eyes set at a slant; and Roger, who for twenty years, since he was seventeen, had been scrupulous in thinking of everyone he met of whatever race or reputation according to that person's individual merits, had smiled at him and thought *beastly bloody kraut*. Expecting to be shocked by the thought, he had only had another, still more surprising: can this be what a fat woman feels when she gets home from a day's shopping, goes up to her bedroom and unhooks her corsets?

He had shaken Herr Becker's hand with extra warmth (for this did not concern Becker, it concerned only himself), then he had crossed to the sunny side of the street and had begun to look at things, which had responded by bursting out of their disguises of familiarity like chestnut buds. He had a lot to do, and he had not exactly forgotten it. He might, though, have wrapped the impending afternoon in a bulky parcel and dropped it into a pool of some opaque substance through which it was now sinking. A Thursday afternoon in March submerged.

The sun was benevolent on Roger's face, the things he

looked at were astonishing, and it occurred to him that he was not going back to the office. He, who in twelve years had never taken the full amount of vacation due to him and had worked at least one day of almost every weekend, was simply not going back to the office, and the idea was so disconcerting that he found no ready response to it. *Odd* was as far as he got, and he vaguely linked it with other oddnesses of the past few weeks, since Felton had won the argument about the symposium on banning nuclear tests and they had turned it down. Roger had argued for the book but he had not fought for it. It was true that it had been proposed by an addle-pated and uninfluential group.

He never used to oversleep and he never used to read the fourth leaders in *The Times*, which bored him, but recently he had taken to doing both, spinning out breakfast however late and having to take a taxi to the office more often than not. And when he got there the weight of boredom he had to push aside before beginning any job, the irritation which rose like bile in his throat at almost every question or interruption, were becoming crippling. Often he could not concentrate. All through the last editorial meeting he had doodled, thinking of nothing but the precise, soaring silhouettes of the cranes at work on a building site in Oxford Street, until Felton and Naomi, noticing his absence, had looked at him in surprise. He had looked back at them, also in surprise, but not at their attitude or his own. What had surprised him, suddenly, had been them. There they were, pushing back chairs and collecting scraps of paper, quite solid, with intestines coiled in their stomachs and unseen hairs growing on their bodies. . . . It had been an effort to come out of the abstraction from which he peered at them like an animal crouching in a cave of shadow as footsteps go by, and when he did come out – come to? – he had shocked himself by saying: Do you know, I've been thinking. In the last twelve years we have published exactly one book without which the world would have been the poorer. Which was rubbish of course.

Roger had stopped in front of the poster saying And Woman Was Created. It struck him that what he would like best at that moment would be to see an amusing film. At that a taxi came by empty, and with a slight interior lurch, as though the pavement under his feet had shifted an inch, he hailed it and told the driver to take him to a cinema in Regent Street which was showing a film starring Fernandel. So what, so what, so what, so what, he hummed to the tune of 'Greensleeves', and the parcel of afternoon settled in the mud at the bottom of the pool. He was free to take the afternoon off if he wished to; if he telephoned the office and told them his intention they would be surprised and inconvenienced but they would have no right to object; the humming, the tautness in his diaphragm, the fixed mean-ingless smile like that of a man walking into the sun, came from his certainty that he was not going to telephone. He had gone on strike.

Pushing into what looked at first like darkness he was dizzy with elation. He found a seat, his eyes greedy on the screen because he was bloody well going to enjoy every second of this now that (good God!) he was doing it. Come Fernandel, he thought, and join the game, to hell with all of it and the lot of them, I've gone on strike from being Roger Paul. Eyes, ears, nose, hands and belly is all I want to be till something else starts growing. And this was even stranger than he thought it because for a long time Roger Paul had resembled closely the man he had chosen to be. *Oh how glad I am*, Nettie, his wife, used to say, *that we at least are nice* (she said it as a joke of course). It had been their pick-me-up after encounters with his family or hers, the one army, the other landed, after listening to remarks like: And blow me down if there wasn't a ruddy great buck nigger sitting in the bar! What that place is coming to I can't imagine. It had been years before Roger could dismiss this kind of thing without a scene, or laugh when one of them said, knowing he voted Labour: Oh but I forgot – of course *you're* a Communist. But later, having gone his own way and been successful in it, he felt secure enough on his own stamping ground to be more amused than angry.

Fernandel came and Roger laughed. He had to laugh because he wanted to. But only a few minutes had gone by before he began to suspect that he was unlucky in this film, that the comedian was not at his best. It was less the lack of occasion for laughter than the deliberate quality of his own response that caused a worm of anxiety to move in the back of his mind. He could still get back to the office not much later than might be explained by some legitimate after-lunch activity (cashing a cheque? buying a tie?), but to give up now would be foolish, he must stay away all afternoon. A florist's shop, and Fernandel was about to wrap a lady's hat instead of some hydrangeas, gazing over his shoulder at a pretty girl passing the window, and did Naomi know that when Stevenson came in about his translation of that Swedish novel he should be told . . . No, this was a waste of time, he must concentrate, and he watched hard. But when, some time later, Fernandel climbed through the wrong bedroom window, Roger had known for too long that so it would be and began to feel the emptiness of the afternoon cinema sucking at his attention. There was only one other person in his row, a girl three seats away.

Will they have noticed yet that . . . Up sprang a paunchy night-capped husband before the goggling eyes of Fernandel who bolted through a door to be trapped in a clothes closet. The girl did not laugh. She sat with hunched shoulders, the big collar of her coat pushing out the tail of hair which sprouted from the back of her head. She felt him looking, glanced and faced the screen again, but her hand went up to smooth the hair round against the side of her neck and she straightened her spine.

Her outline suggested that she was the sort of girl who sat about in coffee bars, remote sometimes, or giggling with other girls delightfully absurd in their dress, their skins so smooth and their eyes so clear behind the masks worn at that time, made of black lines on eyelids and strange pale paint on mouths. To watch girls of this kind made Roger smile with pleasure, but he had never spoken to one. His own women, especially Nettie his wife and Heather who might become his wife, were people like himself because much beauty or silence or strangeness in a woman alarmed him. He had chosen confirmation rather than challenge. When Nettie looked pretty, which she sometimes did, it was at things he shared such as the prospect of a journey abroad or at a meeting with a writer she admired. Neither she nor Heather was a woman whose sex dressed her in mystery like some women to whom he had seen other men fall victim, or like the girls he enjoyed watching across the gulf of years and difference. His had been women he liked and who demanded no abdication from reason (or so he had thought until Nettie went so odd) – and now here was this different kind of girl aware of him in the empty row.

Should he speak to her? He felt reluctant. It would mean coming out of his cave of shadow, girding himself about with personality and being again the man he always was: a well-read man of liberal opinions; a sensitive man who six months ago had parted from his wife with humility because she had stopped loving him and he could, after all, see why (also he had minded less than he had expected); a man living the life he had chosen among people who thought as he did, free to be discriminating in art, to like Negroes, to dislike capitalists, to understand criminals, to sympathise with sexual deviation and to feel constant guilt on his country's behalf towards Cyprus, Israel, Egypt, India (in retrospect) and large parts of Africa; to feel even sharper guilt on the whole world's behalf towards its suicidal image; a man with a mind too good to be fooled; and who, being humble and busy, could not think what he could do about what he saw. He had been to a lot of meetings in his time and had learnt, he felt, their inadequacy. He had never done a bolt (and never would) into Communism, the Catholic Church or a psychiatrist's consulting room. The sort of man he had deliberately set out to be. And who was now sitting in this cinema at 4.15 on a working afternoon, having smiled at Herr Becker and enjoyed thinking *beastly bloody kraut*.

To speak to anyone, then, would mean picking up a burden from which he needed to rest; would be tiring. But worse, he now realised, would be to leave the cinema alone. He could go back to the flat, surprising its weekday emptiness, and at this prospect a skin peeled off part of his mind leaving it raw. He could walk about the streets until the pubs opened – like a madman? He could catch a train and join Heather at the cottage, but he had not enough money on him and anyway with her he would have to be, again, his customary self. Tea, he thought. It cannot be *picking up* to ask a girl to have tea with me, and she will be unknown, I can say I am someone else or perhaps – and here he felt hope stirring – perhaps I can tell her what has happened. And thinking this, Roger, who forgot that he himself did not know what had happened and who was further from feeling desire than he had ever been, had a vision of release, his body lying on a bed in a strange room, a girl getting dressed and going out, leaving him to sleep.

He looked at the screen again, from which Fernandel was absent while a blonde with feathers on her negligée cajoled the fat husband. The girl stood up and began to edge away from him towards the aisle. No decision made, he found himself standing too, out in the aisle on his side and moving parallel with her towards the exit. They reached the door at the same moment and he held it for her, then followed her into the street and took his stand beside her at the nearby bus stop to which she went.

It was easier than he had expected.

You would think, he said, when no bus had come for several minutes, that there was a strike on.

She turned her head, half-smiling, and he saw with excitement that her eyes were amazing, huge and silver-grey between the lines of black.

It wasn't a very good film was it? he went on.

I don't know really. I didn't know it would be all in French.

Her voice whined, the accent just off cockney. Disconcerted by this and by her words Roger saw that she was no more, probably, than eighteen. But he was ashamed of noticing the accent and the hope that she would look at him again made him persist, in spite of her youth.

Don't you find out about films before you go to them? he asked.

Well sometimes, she said. Then, lifting her face and blinking: Don't it seem funny, coming out of the pictures in broad daylight? It leaves you at a loose end, sort of, wondering what to do next.

After that it was easy to suggest a cup of tea in the place across the street, to which she came willingly saying that she supposed she should be getting home really but a cup of tea would be nice, she was parched. Her name, she told him, was Anne.

The hair pulled back from her face was reddish, her chin receded, but the eyes dominated her face and her skin was a child's. Round her neck she wore a velvet ribbon from which

111

hung a cross with green glass at the centre, and her fingernails were dirty.

Why did you go to the cinema this afternoon? he asked.

Oh well, I just went in, she said. I don't start in my new place till Monday, see. Mother said to help her with washing the paint but I've been messing about the house all week, I got fed up. My friend's at work so I couldn't meet her till after, so I just thought why not go up to the West End for a change? Why did you, anyway?

I happened to have a free afternoon.

Where do you work?

The BBC, said Roger (because it was nearby).

Are you in the television?

No – no, in sound radio.

I like the telly sometimes but I'm not mad about it like my friend. We used to go ice-skating every week, Wednesdays, but now it's all I can do to get her out.

Is skating what you like to do best? he asked, thinking yes, that would suit those eyes.

Well I do sometimes but I wouldn't say best. I like dancing too, and I like reading, I'm funny like that.

Good, said Roger hopefully, preparing to understand the charm, for her, of books he would probably despise. I read a lot too, he said.

I think it's ever so nice. I take three books every week, *True Story*, *Mademoiselle* and *She*.

Oh, said Roger.

They sipped tea in silence for a moment, until Anne said that the tea was ever so hot and Roger answered yes.

Then, making an effort, remembering unread columns in many newspapers picturing lives unlike his own: Do you like jazz? he said.

That old stuff! My boyfriend's mad about it, he is really. All those old records, they all sound the same to me.

But you ought to like jazz, said Roger feeling trapped. I thought you all did.

All who?

You gay young things, he said, and knew how old she saw him and how dull; knew too, with a mixture of disappointment and relief, that he could tell her nothing.

After that he found it hard to think of things to say but Anne did not seem to mind. She turned her great eyes on the other people in the tea shop, commenting sometimes on their appearance, and when Roger muttered about an appointment she said thank you for the tea and ran across the road to the bus stop without looking back, while Roger turned down a side street and hurried away, where to?

Depression went with him now. Why had he not telephoned the office and spared himself conjecture as to what they must be supposing, and why was this all he could find to do? Where had it gone, whatever had been prompting him to withdraw into his skin and by so doing to shrug off Roger Paul? Stillness and silence were to get him into something or out of something, the bright clear solid objects about him were to tell him something – and here he was, elation ebbing and conscience beginning to bump at his heels. Those cranes, he thought, I've been wanting to look at them, I'll walk past them now.

The cranes, rearing into the sky from perches at rooftop level, were working with the hesitant precision of craftsmen on a tricky job. They swung great girders from one height to another, tons of metal looking up there like matchsticks – but now to the indifferent film and the girl was added a pneumatic drill working on a nearer part of the site, sawing at Roger's brain so that he squinted and began to feel sick. Naomi loves panics, he thought, she will probably call the police, and anyway what shall I tell them when they ask where I have been? This must be why people become alcoholics or turn up in Glasgow not knowing who they are, and all I have done is go to the cinema. Perhaps, he thought, if I move nearer the drill, into the thickest of the clangour, I shall find a still centre as the man who works it must or he would go mad. But the nearer he moved the more it battered and vibrated and screamed into his skull. He tightened his muscles, bending slightly forward as though against lashing rain. I can't even have a proper nervous breakdown, he thought. I must get out of this, Christ I must get out of it, and he turned and almost ran down the street, frightened and angry. I'm not on strike, he thought, I'm on the run.

The street ended at a corner of Regent's Park, which when he reached it was almost empty. Only a few people were walking dogs across the generous country-seeming spaces in the fading light. Roger sat down on a bench to light a cigarette, then leant forward, elbows on knees, and stared at the toffee papers and husks of monkey nuts on the path between his feet. Tired, he felt, and thirsty in spite of the tea, and he could no longer prevent himself visualising details of the consternation his absence must be causing. Stevenson, the translator – oh Lord, he remembered, the wretched man was coming all the way up from Bognor for the appointment.

As he sat staring, there came the scuff of feet on the path. He looked up and saw an old woman approaching, on her head a wide-brimmed straw hat trimmed with roses once pink, the man's overcoat which flapped round her feet secured over her stomach with two safety-pins. She paused, started to go on, then turned as though deciding to claim her rights after all and lowered herself painfully to sit at the far end of the bench. Turning her back on Roger and inching a little towards him, she drew from under the coat an untidy parcel wrapped in newspaper. This she began slowly to unpack on the end of the bench sheltered from Roger's sight. He leant forward to see what was coming out: an empty sardine tin, two crushed fronds of ostrich feather, the heel of a loaf, a broken photograph frame, a cutlet bone, a set of false teeth, a wrinkled apple with one bite browning in its side and a roll of fresh green ribbon.

The old woman flattened the paper carefully and arranged her hoard upon it, changing the position of the objects sometimes as though there were a correct order which she knew but had temporarily forgotten. Then, the ribbon in her hand, she hesitated, cocked her head as though listening and suddenly swung round to stare straight into Roger's face. Hers he had not seen till then, shaded as it was by the brim of her hat and the locks of cinder-coloured hair hanging forward over her cheeks. Looking at him, she pushed the hair back at one side and he now met an eye of extraordinary innocence, almost completely round, pale blue and like a baby's in its accepting, unwatchful gaze. Her skin was either brown or filthy, her small toothless mouth an upturned crescent, a permanent smile sunk between nose and chin. Her innocent, smiling interrogation was endless and he felt that he must speak.

That, he said softly, is a pretty piece of ribbon.

For a moment she did not answer. Then, turning back to her belongings she said in a clear, prim old lady's voice: Mind your own fucking business you bleeding papist bastard.

I'm sorry, muttered Roger, the blood rushing to his forehead, and as he got up he kept his eyes lowered, seeing only her foot sticking out from under the coat: the torn black canvas shoe and the purple knob of her ankle, the skin crisscrossed with dry white cracks.

The light was going. Soon the park would be shut. In a scared effort at common sense he decided that he had time to walk once round the park putting his thoughts in order and then would go home. But when he reached the more open, wilder part with the zoo to the north and water lying misty on his left, it was already nearly dark and he could hear the park-keepers' whistles in the distance and their calls of *All out*. He stood among trees. A keeper came riding a bicycle along a path near him, blowing his whistle as he pedalled, and Roger without intent drew back against the trunk of an elm tree and was not seen. The keeper vanished in the dusk, one last dog-owner hurried in his wake and in a few minutes the minatory whistles ceased, somewhere out of sight gates were chained, men lit cigarettes and went off duty. Roger, frozen against his tree, felt the ache in the palms of his hands which he recognised from night patrols during the war. It was hard to believe that if he were now caught nothing very terrible would happen.

He noticed for the first time that a wind had risen on this warm evening and that a moon was already in the sky. The silence was vast, contained within the encircling city's hum but not diminished by it, and when he began to walk again the swish of his feet in the grass sounded loud. The wind ran overhead and he was alone.

It was not elation coming back to him, though he felt again the tautness he had experienced early in the afternoon, and that a purpose was within his reach. To be here in the night park where no one ever came – or so he supposed, ignorant of those who clamber over fences with girls or for darker purposes – to be in the centre of it all but alone: perhaps he had come without alcohol or forgetting what he had been seeking, had shed enough of his surface to uncover the cause of his flight. He was unwilling to turn his attention upon himself (no, it was not elation, it was fear), but light had gone, sound had gone, people had gone: there was nothing else to claim it. I am alone here, he thought, nothing else is here but what cannot change, and I have got to look at it.

The wind was rushing faster between the still moon and the still grass which was too short to sway with it. It poured through the darkness, pressing Roger's clothes against his body, but he did not feel cold, only empty. He sat down on the grass, his knees up, his arms resting across his knees and his forehead on his arms, while between the moon and the earth the wind came flooding over him. I have failed in love, he thought, and I have failed in action. Understanding, honesty, guilt: they are only sops I have thrown to the monster as I backed into my hole, they are not enough and never can be. And whatever I uncover I shall not change because in all this space and darkness here I am, so inadequate yet as solid as a pebble. This, he thought with interest rather than horror, would be the time to die. There would be nothing to it, it would only be one short step further, and he saw clearly the litter left by a dead animal: a skeleton collapsed and tangled in grass. Then for a little while he saw nothing and felt nothing. He was asleep, almost, having come unexpectedly but without surprise to the end of where he could go.

Perhaps fifteen minutes later he lifted his head. So that's that, he said aloud, rising stiffly from the unaccustomed position. So long as one knows. . . . And it had, indeed, brought him to a strange flat calm, as though from here he need not worry.

It was not difficult to get out of the park. His legs were long and he came by chance to a place where the hedge, with its core of wire netting, was low. His hands, he noticed in the bus, were scratched but only slightly. The telephone was ringing as he came up the stairs to the door of his flat, and although it stopped as he put his key in the lock it began again ten minutes later while he was pouring his second drink. Naomi's agitation was so great that at first she was incoherent. *Is it him? Is it Roger?* he heard Felton ask behind her, and he said quietly: Yes it's me, I'm here and I'm all right. Then as she began again, quack quack quack: For Christ's sake leave me alone, he shouted, and crashed the receiver down. His voice was so wild that when next morning he arrived punctually at the office they looked away from his face and neither of them, then or ever, asked him what had happened on that Thursday afternoon.

AN UNAVOIDABLE DELAY

It was on a railway train and in one compartment were five people. One a Rumanian dozing against the window, three Americans, father, mother and daughter with so much matching and expensive luggage that it filled both the racks and the remaining corner seat, and one a small English-woman with smooth dark hair called Rose, very careful not to look like an Englishwoman abroad, her dress neither of flowered cotton nor full in the skirt and her shoes elegant with quite high heels. The Englishwoman was sad, not only because a holiday was ending. In her bag were three letters from her husband which she had found waiting for her at Ljubljana, one of four pages, one of seven pages and one of twelve pages. She had skimmed the short one, looked at the beginnings and ends of the others and said to herself: There will be plenty of time to read them on the train. She had not done so yet. She knew what was in them.

To talk would prevent her thinking, but the Rumanian was languageless among them and the Americans, who had square right-thinking faces, were reserved because it is so hard to tell with foreigners. The mother and daughter wore little suits as though for drinking coffee with friends in the morning and pretty uncreased blouses of white lawn, almost a miracle after travelling a fortnight in Yugoslavia. The father was a doctor concerned with health in industry, returning from an international conference to which, with his family, he had been invited. In other compartments were other doctors, English, French and Scandinavian, all contented after such a good conference though some still with indigestion.

What was in the letters, Rose knew, was that if she left Neville he would throw up his job, start drinking again and (in the twelve-page letter, probably) put his head in the gas oven. Going away by herself had not worked, it seemed, although it had been wonderful. Halfway through the second week, in Dubrovnik, she had begun to flirt with a handsome Yugoslav architect and this she had especially enjoyed. She had stopped only when the architect, growing confident, had made that remark about Englishwomen not being cold really, not with the right men, but what a misfortune for them to be married to English husbands. Rose always hoped that foreigners would not make this remark but they usually did, particularly when on a beach or in the evening she wore her hair loose and not coiled high at the back of her head. The architect looked particularly fatuous when he made it, Rose grew quite angry; after all, she thought, thousands no *millions* of English husbands were perfectly splendid and just because she happened . . . anyway she saw then that to go on with this architect would be worse than full skirts, flowered cotton and flat sandals, it would be too banal, not to be thought of. After that she stayed near the other friends she had made, married couples or women, whose delicate assumption that she was a little prudish in an attractive English way was fortifying. Warm-hearted, they judged her, but chaste. And so she was, after all, as people go.

There had been a great quarrel before she started on this holiday alone and she had hoped that now Neville would say that she had gone too far, and mean it. At the beginning she used to think: If only, when I am beastly, he would beat me; but now for several years she had thought further than that, she had thought: Oh why won't he make up his mind to throw me out? But he would not be unfair or unkind or unfaithful, he would only go on being the nice unhappy man she should never have married, and seeing from the short letter that this time, too, he was crying for her, she had spent an almost sleepless night in Ljubljana having sober thoughts. After all, she had thought, I would miss the house, it would probably be more difficult than I think to have no money, our friends are nice. I can *do* more, she had thought – take up painting again, perhaps. But chiefly she had thought: It is all my fault and anyway we are getting older, surely as the years go by I will mind less and less. Think of all the little boys and girls who haven't *got* any lovely rice pudding . . . lucky little bastards, thought Rose, as always, but there was something in it, she supposed. And so she sat in the train very sadly and when the American daughter asked the father if they were near the frontier yet, Rose, to her horror, nearly began to cry. Oh if only the train were going the other way!

In the corridor outside this compartment stood one Greek doctor. He felt less important than some of the others and had been too polite to grab a seat but he looked sadly sometimes at the seat beside Rose on which the American suitcases were piled. No wonder, because it was to be a long journey. At first Rose had thought the cases were his and were to keep him a place while he took the air in the corridor by choice. But now, when her thoughts drove her out to stand in the corridor herself for a change and she found how well the Greek doctor spoke French and English, she learnt that it was not his baggage, no, but the right-thinking Americans'.

When she looked at them then she became almost alarmed and so did the Greek, they were so alike, father, mother and daughter, all three square and clean and conscious of their rightness. They were not people who would do such a thing and yet they had, it was against nature. Angry she said: 'No, they must not, it is too bad'; then loudly to the Greek: 'Why I thought *that* was your seat, have you not got one? Why did you not say before and we would have put these cases in the corridor.' So the American father had no alternative, and after that it seemed cooler in the compartment.

So Rose and the Greek doctor sat side by side and his name was Paul. He was short but not too fat and although most of his hair was grey his eyebrows were black. He had a friendly face, thought Rose, and how delightful that he was eager to talk.

'I am not really concerned with health in industry,' he said, 'only some of my research touches on it and I have written papers which have been published in London even, and Paris.' He was proud of these papers, he brought them in soon, and Rose thought that probably this was the first international conference to which he had ever been invited. 'I envy you your profession,' said Rose.

'It is an interesting life,' said Paul, 'but what I would like to do best is to be a painter.'

'And do you ever paint?' she asked.

'Yes,' he said, 'one year I painted all the summer, the first summer I discovered this wish. I painted and neglected my work until my wife grew anxious. But I have two children, the responsibility is great, so now I must paint only at weekends.'

'I sometimes paint too,' said Rose, and when he was most interested to hear this and questioned her about it, she hoped that he would never come to London and ask to see the few bad paintings she had once done. But as she talked of them and they sounded good it occurred to her that his, which also sounded good, might be just as bad.

So they talked, Paul and Rose, about painting; and both if they had been forced to choose only one painter would have chosen Renoir. This was because they had been much in the sun in Yugoslavia, drinking wine and eating fruit. Also both if they had been forced to choose only one composer would have chosen at this moment Schubert, though at many other times they would have chosen Bach. They turned towards each other smiling, each so pleased to find a companion for this long journey, and Rose especially pleased because not only was he ready to talk but she liked him and there could be no tiresomeness, the train was carrying her along and besides he spoke so freely and fondly of his wife and children. Until he gets off at Milan, she thought, I will try to keep him by me. Sometimes they spoke in French instead of English to show themselves superior to the Americans who could not, and sometimes they were kind to the Rumanian but he was nervous, going for the first time out of his country to a youth congress, also he had a headache. The three Americans appeared not to listen but sometimes they smiled a little tightly.

The journey went on through the rest of the morning and some of the afternoon, by the sea or not, until they looked at watches and saw that soon the train would stop at Venice.

'Have you visited Venice?' asked Paul.

'Only once and then only for three days. It is the tragedy of my life.'

'And that too is like me!' he exclaimed. 'Only once and only for three days, and now we shall be in Venice but only for twenty minutes and only in the station.'

The Americans were getting out at Venice, they were taking the opportunity, and now the father spoke to Rose: 'That is too bad, from the station you can't even see anything.'

The train began to make a different noise, it was coming onto the long thin causeway and water began to be on either side.

'This is silly,' said Rose, 'to be in Venice and not to be in Venice.' And she was silent, feeling how silly it was, Venice no more than big letters on a station sign and tomorrow Neville on the platform not caring in the least about her holiday, only anxious to begin again at once on how could she. When she next spoke it was abrupt: 'I think I shall get out,' she said.

'We are only here for twenty minutes,' said Paul.

'Right out. With my luggage. And take another train tomorrow. I can send a telegram saying unavoidably delayed.' Saying this Rose began to tremble with excitement, she wanted so much to do it; and looking at Paul as she spoke she surprised in her mind the words (quickly brushed away) 'Now will he do it too?' Perhaps it was only the way the American mother refrained from catching her daughter's eye that signalled the presence of those words in the compartment.

And Paul was excited too. 'You are right,' he said, 'you are quite right, that is what should be done, we do not do these things in life often enough. But I have people meeting me in Milan, it is official.'

'Poor you,' she said warmly, 'what a shame.' And she realised that she might feel a little forlorn, all alone in Venice, no one to have dinner with, even.

'I could send a telegram?' he said.

'Oh but should you, if it is official?' she said carefully, not looking at the American mother.

'And it is Sunday,' he said in despair. 'Their office will be shut.'

'It would never do,' said Rose. 'If they did not get your telegram and came to meet you, how rude they would think you.'

'What shall I do?' he asked, turning right round to her.

'You must think what you would feel about it if you were them.'

'I should think I was most rude.'

'Yes indeed,' she said; and was surprised that her heart sank.

'But I could telephone the director's house?' he questioned.

'No no,' she laughed, 'you must not make me responsible for this wildness.'

'I shall telephone,' he said to them all. The Americans were busy with luggage and did not smile.

How sunny was the platform at Venice and how solid after the train, and also how strange the two of them together, walking not sitting. Many of the doctors were getting off the train, they were taking the opportunity, and although they were anxious about porters Paul called to them: 'Look, I have changed my mind, it is an impulse.' They smiled and looked at Rose and an old doctor with a beard smiled even more, but kindly. The Americans had disappeared.

'To telephone,' said Paul, clapping his hands, 'that must be first. If you will excuse me I will do it now and meet you on the steps outside the station.'

'And I,' she said, 'will change a traveller's cheque because I have no money left, not a cent,' and this was true. So she went alone through marble halls to where it said Exchange and when she got there the lady in glasses behind the counter said: 'What is this? I cannot change this cheque.'

'Why, what is wrong?' cried Rose. 'These are ordinary cheques from my bank, I have used them in Yugoslavia for three weeks.'

'In Yugoslavia I do not know, but here you cannot. They are good cheques but there is nothing stamped here on the back, the bank has forgotten. You cannot change them here.'

'Then where can I change them?'

'You cannot,' said the lady.

'But this is absurd, I must, I have no money.'

'Perhaps at Thomas Cook's,' said the bored lady.

So Rose went out on the steps and hardly noticed the Grand Canal. A pretty pickle, she thought, what will he suppose? Perhaps I am to be punished – but the sun beat down and rippled off water onto faded brick, so she quickly thought: At Thomas Cook's it will be all right, it must be. And she began to look about her, her cheeks pink and her eyes bright although she did not know it.

At once a man came to her, wearing a smart uniform and a cap with Danieli written on it.

'Thank you no,' said Rose, smiling. 'I am looking for a cheap hotel, two single bedrooms in a cheap hotel.' Yes, she thought, there can be no question about *that*: two single bedrooms. At that moment here came Paul breathless, the telephone booths were all engaged, would she mind if he were a few minutes more? No, she would not mind, she would try to find a room for him as well as for herself.

'You are with the gentleman?' asked the man from the Danieli.

'We have been in the same train.'

'There are no single rooms in Venice,' he replied, 'no single rooms at all,' and he turned to three friends all in hotel uniforms and they answered no, no single rooms at all.

'Then two double rooms,' she said, 'but it must be in a cheap hotel.'

'That is a waste of money,' said one man. 'Why two double rooms, why not one double room?'

All the men were grinning, it was a small persecution, but the sun beat down and rippled off water and Rose felt far away and safe. To say, she thought, that we are not married will make them grin worse, so she said in Italian, slowly and carefully: 'Because the gentleman and I are not in love.'

At this the men laughed aloud but became friendly, and Danieli shouted to another man, a thin man with no uniform but the cap: 'Nazionale,' shouted Danieli, 'you have two single rooms?'

'Yes,' said Nazionale, 'yes, the last two in Venice.'

'How much?' she asked, and the price was not too high.

Then Rose sat on her suitcase in the sun and talked to the men, now serious, about the tourist season and the Biennale. Only for one night, she thought vaguely, and I shall pay for it when I get home. But her dreamy feeling of elation was not, perhaps, quite in keeping with the sober thought.

When Paul came they went to their hotel nearby, up to their rooms (not at all bad), washed, changed and met politely in the hall.

'One thing,' said Rose, 'it is a bore, I must go to Thomas Cook's,' and she told her tale. 'Shall I meet you somewhere later?' she asked to make her independence clear, but he said no, he would come with her. So together they went in a *vaporetto* down the Grand Canal and began to laugh, but Rose was not quite easy about those cheques. And at Thomas Cook's it was worse because that lady in the glasses had been right, it was impossible to change the cheques. Such argument, such rage and pleading, but all they said was: 'The British Consul, maybe he will lend you money but it is Sunday, he will not be there.'

'Oh what shall I do?' said Rose. 'I am so sorry, it is a scandal, my bank is mad.'

'Yes, it is a very bad scandal,' said Paul. 'You must be very angry with your bank when you are at home, even take away your account, but for now do not worry for I have some dollars and I will lend them to you.' He said it in a way at once reassuring, he believed her and that she would pay him back, he would not think of it as a claim on her, but still she went on to make him certain, managing to blush and even almost to cry, although she found it hard to blush when she was guiltless and all was turning out so well.

In the Piazza San Marco they sat, and then in the Piazzetta, ate ices, drank coffee and Cinzano, threw grain to birds, strolled here, strolled there, too happy to be there to look further. Rose had quite stopped thinking. Like skaters the screaming swifts sliced and sliced at the air growing lavender-coloured, the pale moon floated up, quite round: 'Look, even a full moon for us, it is too much.'

Painting they talked of again, and Greece (he forgave her Cyprus and she gave it him), and something of the people round them and much of Paul's life. Rose did not wish to talk of hers and need not have worried, she did not get the chance. Paul's wife, he said, was born Italian, in the war he had suffered for this, he had suffered more than any other Greek, he said, in so many words.

'And your wife too?' asked Rose.

'I suppose so,' he said, surprised. 'It was not her fault, she is a good woman, but for me it was terrible.'

More than any other Greek? wondered Rose, and found by questioning that in the war nothing much had happened to him but this suffering, which was a relief but how strange that it should be so bad. Bad it was, no doubt, and even dangerous; but more than *any other Greek*? No, it was strange. And Rose gazed at Paul in admiration, she began to see that he was not just a friendly well-informed man with plenty to talk about; he was a different kind of man, unlike those she knew. He loved himself without trouble and had never thought, it seemed, that he should not.

Then Paul went on to tell of his other suffering, his great great love which, when his wife discovered it he had to sacrifice, it nearly killed him. After that he knew that if he were not a good husband he was still, he always would be, a good *chef de famille*, it was for that he had given up his love. But because of it he now had a bad heart, yes, a really bad heart physically, and grief, he knew, had done it. Placing his hand on his ribs he said his colleagues told him (and he knew it himself) that if he were not careful all the time he would fall down dead. Goodness, thought Rose. Her eyes grew brighter as she gazed at him, she was so enchanted by this heart. Now that is doing it in style, she thought, and the more she nearly giggled the more she was enchanted.

Where to dine? they wondered, neither of them knew, but here came the old doctor with a beard, most genial after early dinner. 'Aha,' he said, 'you must go to my little place across the Rialto Bridge,' and he described. 'You will like it there,' he said, and he was right. A street, an alley, a small bridge, steps, another alley becoming a passage – and can this be it, this door? It has no sign. 'Come, let us be brave and push.' Paul went ahead, the door opened into kitchen steam and garlic; this way, through here, and there was a little garden with high walls round it, vine trellis above, a window in one wall with the arches of the fish market beyond. It was a most delicious dinner and Paul ate, but Rose had begun to feel sick, she could not eat.

At dinner, when in arguing she made a wide gesture, Paul caught her hand and held it on the table, it was the first touch; but, thought Rose, how terrible if this sickness is not just tiredness and excitement but something I ate in Ljubljana. For fear it might be, and it was growing strong, she quickly agreed when he urged: 'Shall we go?' She wished to do many things in Venice that night, to wander in many places, hardly to sleep, but so strong was the sickness growing that when he said: 'You are tired, such a long journey, it is best we go back to the hotel,' when he said that: Yes, she thought, and the sooner the better, how mortifying.

'I love to go down these dark alleys,' said Paul, 'let us go down this one,' and his arm was across her shoulders. In the darkness he kissed her neck for she turned away her face thinking: It would be less terrible here in a very dark alley than in a light one, but better in the hotel. 'I really am tired,' said Rose, not moving her lips much, 'I would like to go back.' On the *vaporetto* she stood close to the rail to be safe, Paul against her (the crowd pressure an excuse). Now this would be shame and horror, thought Rose, but nothing happened quite.

Safe in her bedroom, how strange, it began to go away. He stood by her door. 'May I come back to say good night?' he asked softly and she did not answer, smiling and looking down. She did not think, only that this was better, it was really going. But she cleaned her teeth quickly because to be caught doing that is so . . .

Then on her naked body she put her dressing-gown and went smiling, not thinking, to the window to see what was the great noise. Perhaps it was because she was now so very tired that at this moment only the noise interested her. It was an open-air cinema, a western – and oh the soundtrack! no wonder these rooms were cheap. 'Look!' said Rose when Paul came sidling round the door, 'if we lean out of my window we can see a film, a western.' 'So,' he said, and came beside her, his arm round her waist, and they leant together; but feeling her naked under her dressing-gown Paul turned her roughly towards him and kissed her on the mouth and this time she did not turn away her face. They kissed a long kiss, the dressing-gown unbuttoning, and Rose thought how odd that kissing should make sickness go quite away instead of making it worse, while Paul murmured: 'May I, may I please, oh come, come to the bed.' His heart was beating so, oh his heart! What, she thought suddenly, does one do with a Greek doctor dead in one's bed in Venice? Goodness, thought Rose.

Which it was, it was surprising because surely she had mostly been thinking him funny? It was very good and seemed the right thing to be doing without a doubt in a narrow bed with a hard mattress. They knew each other very well, it seemed, and after they had made love they found they loved each other so that they had to say it, even knowing it was only true at that time. 'I love you, no, don't laugh, I know, but

I love you,' he said as he stroked her body, gazing and stroking. And she put her arms round his neck and kissed him with joy saying, 'I love you too.' It was very good. 'Did you expect this on the steps?' he said. 'What a waste, two rooms.' But they agreed that then it would have been impossible to think of one, it would have been shocking, for although they both knew now that earlier they had expected, no, intended it, perhaps, at the time they had not known they knew. What is it? wondered Rose, nearly asleep, turning her head so that her lips were against his shoulder. It is not that he is a 'better' lover – and she shied from the memory of Neville's conscientiously professional embraces. It must be just that he *loves* women as warmly as he loves himself and I – good God, I do believe that I love men.

So that was almost all they saw of Venice because in the morning they were too lazy for more than the Piazza San Marco where they saw the American family sitting at Florian's and very clean. 'Now,' said Paul, 'I must say good morning. I was with them at the conference, to pass by would be rude.' Bowing he hurried to them between tables to shake hands, Rose there as though by chance. 'Yes,' he said, 'I found a hotel without trouble and so, it seems, did Miss Rose.' Oh dear, those women's faces left no room for misunderstanding, while embarrassed the father smiled, nodded and stared up at the campanile. But Rose did not mind, she was pleased, she was wearing a prettier dress than either of those women and what were they to her as she stood in the sun?

Resting before packing, when they made love again, he asked her for the first time about her husband. 'I am going to leave him,' she said. 'It is my fault, he is a good man and I have tortured him to death almost, I should never have married him. He makes love a battle always, and he hasn't the courage to win it.'

'Does he not love you?' asked Paul, not understanding.

'Oh yes, he loves me, but with him love is a question of proving something – it is always a worry, it has made me too unkind.'

'He must be a fool,' said Paul. He did not want to talk about any suffering but his own. 'Feel my heart,' he said, and it was indeed beating much too fast. 'I give up smoking,' he said, 'and I give up drinking and I give up walking up many stairs, but this I will not give up, I would like to die like this.' Which, she thought lazily, was all very well, only luckily he stayed alive. And when they talked again it was again about him and Rose did not mind, she liked it. He is wonderful, she thought. Even when he bowed his head in sorrow speaking of his country and how great the struggle, how great the poverty, he lifted his head soon to say proudly: 'It is because we are undisciplined, we think only of ourselves; why worry about a better world for my children when it is my life I am living?' (But he loved his children passionately, they were himself.) It is strange, thought Rose, that a man so full of self can love women so openly and kindly. Perhaps he has never been crossed by a woman all his life, cherished man-child, respected husband, adored lover, absolute father, so that he can love women without any grudge.

They caught another train that afternoon not very early and found a small compartment with no one in it (it was a journey of wonders) so that they sat embracing all the way. For one week, they said, they would think of each other all the time and for the next week half of the time and after that less often, but they would not forget. Rose indeed would not forget. She did not now have to think (or to try not to think) about her homecoming, she would have time to think about it later and she knew now in what way it would be sad and that it would look after itself. At Milan she borrowed more money from Paul for the journey and did not mind leaving him, she still felt so warm and happy; but he seeing her silence thought it grief, naturally he thought it, he would. When at last he kissed her goodbye he was most moved by the grief he thought she had at losing him.

'Don't be sad,' said Paul tenderly, 'don't be sad, be happy. Think that you have given me much joy.'

When Rose began to laugh he was surprised, he was almost hurt, but she gave him a great kiss and said: 'Darling Paul, I won't be sad I promise. I love you, darling Paul.'

So that journey ended much better than it began.

AN ISLAND

'But don't you see, the important thing – the enormously important thing – is *not* commitment. You go on about commitment in a political sense as though that were what mattered. God, it annoys me! Because . . .'

'Darling, you are being a bore. Do stop being such a bore for one little tiny minute.'

'My wife is drunk. Do you find that, Lucy – George, I mean? Do you find that when your wife gets drunk it all comes out? This little itch to *get at* the male? Listen, ever since that bloody awful party at the Schmidts', and that was only three months after we got married, you've been getting at me whenever you've got drunk. You sound like those women who resent being underneath in bed so much. . . .'

'Martin, if you're going to start on the half-baked Freudian kick we'd better be going. It's time we went, anyway.'

'Nonsense, it's only midnight, they don't want us to go yet. You don't want us to go yet, do you, Lucy?'

'Martin, if you don't come I'll go without you.'

'All right then, go.'

'Throw him out when you've had enough,' said Madeleine Cross to her hostess, in what she thought was a cool, amused voice. She picked up her purse and was on the front-door steps before she realised that she had left her long green gloves on the arm of her chair and was still holding an empty wine-glass. If Lucy doesn't put the gloves in his pocket, she thought, I can pick them up tomorrow. I've remembered them and I've thought what to do about them. I'm pretty sober, you see.

Her heels went tap-tap tap-tap on the pavement in a marching rhythm. How fast she was walking, and steadily, too. She could change the rhythm if she wanted to, walk slower or faster, or even make her feet go the other way, take the wine-glass back and leave it on their doorstep. If she wished to decide to do that, she could: it was just that she did not wish to. And if she might not have had to think about her walking in quite this way, supposing that she had been sober, at least it showed how almost sober she was that she recognised it. Certain things about being a little drunk were amusing: feeling sober because of it, then seeing that feeling sober meant being drunk, then recognising that seeing that feeling sober meant being drunk was really sober. . . . Goodness! It was like peeling an onion. Madeleine smiled indulgently at her drunkenness, marching in the wrong direction through the moonlight, holding the wine-glass upright in front of her.

Well, what a relief! Why had she never done it before?

The house she had left stood in a square. To reach the street which would take her into a busier street where a taxi might be found, she should have turned to the right outside the door instead of to the left, so now she would have to walk right round the square instead of along one side of it. Martin would expect her to notice her mistake, to falter and to go back past the house: he would be standing by the window, laughing. So tap-tap went her heels, all the way round, back to the side on which the house stood, and out at the corner into the street. Ha!

He had been so childish, getting riled like that by George. As soon as he began to splutter 'the important thing – the enormously important thing' he was bound to make a fool of himself, he always did. Soon he would be saying 'the point is' and never getting to it. Now he would probably be remembering that she never put money into her evening purse, and he would not be worrying, he would be laughing, because he did not know that she happened to feel like walking – she would walk even if she had some money. At this rate she would be home in half an hour, and the air smelt of lime trees in flower – 'Ach, linden Duft. . . .' The soaring line of Mahler's little lime flower song was running through her head, but she was not going to sing, oh no. Drunk she might be, but not so drunk as that.

The middle of the night in a quiet residential neighbourhood: no one about and not a taxi to be seen. The summer air was silky on her face, light glinted on the wine-glass, and how pretty it was: a simple, tulip-shaped glass with a plain stem and a rather broad foot, the best shape for a wine-glass – and when you came to look at it, in itself a *perfect* shape. She held it up in front of her, ran a finger round its rim and down the curve of the bowl. What a pity that transparency hadn't been invented at one blow. They had experimented for centuries with the stuff, getting there slowly, painfully, after thousands of near misses, and think what a miracle it would have been if they had hit on the right mixture straightaway, so that one man in Alexandria or somewhere could have seen the impossible blossoming as he breathed into it: pure transparency, nothingness embodied. It's so beautiful, she thought, so really beautiful. I'm glad I've still got it.

'All right then, go. . . .' And she – she! – had got up and gone. He had not expected it for one moment, but he had seen her skirt whisk round the door, heard her steps in the hall and the front door shutting (*not* slamming) and the tap-tap on the pavement – going in the wrong direction, of course, that was a pity. But it was also funny, and she giggled at the thought of it. She had looked such a fool, and he had waited, leaning on the windowsill, she was sure, expecting her to come back, and when he had seen her silhouetted by a street lamp, turning out of the square after all, he (or George or Lucy) must have said, 'Good God, she *has* gone, too!' Had he returned to his chair and started pontificating again, or would he follow her at once? It didn't matter.

She had never done such a thing before, or even wanted to, and why should she, married as she was to a man who suited her so well? She did not think, now, of him and her together, because she did not need to. His name in her mind meant his high forehead, his deep-set brown eyes, his long bony nose and his mouth turning down at the corners when he smiled, and when she saw that, there it all was. They had been married for three years and neither of them had the least doubt about it. Sometimes it occurred to Madeleine that the

142

extra thing between them, in addition to their tastes in common and the comfort of their bodies together – the thing which had made them fall in love at once and which made it impossible to imagine living with anyone else – was that the parts of each of them which had not changed since childhood happened to be at home together. 'That's what compatibility is,' she had said once. He was a black-and-white man, like George with his political commitment but about other things, and she was the only person who knew how black-and-white he was – how genuinely puzzled he was by people who used minor dishonesties like saying they were out when they were in; how painfully distressed by any form of callousness. Other people would have thought that he exaggerated, so he had learnt to recognise the boundaries of naïvety and over-sensitivity, and to avoid crossing them too often and too openly with other people. With her it was all right, just as it was all right with him for her to cry over hurt animals, or to love sea-shells so much. They used no little language, but she could see why other lovers did: like herself and Martin they had no façades on the sides they presented to each other so that everything was too familiar to be ridiculous. And come to think of it, she and Martin did call porridge 'podgers', which came from her childhood. . . . 'If you don't get your podgers you surely will die,' she sometimes sang as she stirred it, and very silly *that* would sound to anybody but him.

She did not exactly think of these things as she marched along: she just saw his face, and oh no my dear, she said in her head to Lucy. No, you haven't been witnessing the first crack in the Cross ménage. He's mine, the silly ass, and it's all George's fault anyway, for pouring such monstrous drinks. Martin never pontificates unless he's drunk, and he never starts on that old Freudian kick unless he's *stewed*, and you know how rarely he gets stewed. It's not that *veritas* we've hit on, it's nothing to do with him.

But although she saw that, and suspected for a moment that she would soon see the possibility of Martin's being hurt as well as angry, and of her own regret, it did not seem important. To say out loud that he was a bore had been brutal, even if it was not true – but she only laughed when she remembered it, feeling pleased with herself, for who would have suspected *her*, so lazy and so willing to please, of such sudden dissidence? Love, she thought. What a tangle. And she danced a few steps at being alone in the quiet street. The branch of a tree reached over a wall above a lamp-post, its leaves still young and fresh, a brilliant theatrical green in the artificial light. Between the lamp-posts the sky reappeared, a deep purple-blue where the moon was suspended straight overhead, but rusty pink with London's glow where it came down at the end of the street to outline the roofs. She need not go home. She could decide to walk all night, make for the river or Hampstead Heath, because she was not tired and her shoes were comfortable in spite of their heels. It was odd that the determined rhythm of her walking seemed so definitely aimed towards home. Here, for instance, was the busy street. If she turned to the left it would take her, after a long walk, into the City which at night would be deserted and strange – perhaps a single black cat sitting on the steps of the National

Bank of Argentina. . . . But her feet went on, tap-tap along the street in the direction of home, and she held the wine-glass nearer her body so that the few people she now passed would not notice it.

Soon she had to cross the busy street – not busy now, only brightly lit – at a point where it divided, islanding a church with a graveyard thrusting a wedge into the traffic. Between church and graveyard a narrow passage ran, a short cut for pedestrians. Tap-tap she went, past the iron post which stood in the passage's entrance, into the shadow thrown by the trees in the graveyard, where it was very still: so still that it was like stepping into a different element and her feet slowed, then stopped. There were only a few cars passing behind her and ahead of her, but even if the street had been full the stillness would surely have been here. It was an island. The smell of lime trees was again heavy in the air, leaves rustled very slightly, and after the lights of the street it seemed dark so that she shut her eyes for a moment in order to see better when she opened them again. Sure enough, it was not dark, because of the moon; it was a patchwork of shadow and dim silver light, and when she went close to the railings between passage and graveyard, rested one knee on the little brick wall in which they were set and peered through them, she could see that the man who had mowed the grass had been careless, leaving an irregular ridge uncut here and there between his coming and going: that was the extra smell, of course – new-mown grass. The graves had become history, not mortality, flat under the lawn, with a few eighteenth-century headstones left there for decoration rather than in memory of people.

Carefully she stood the wine-glass on the railing, between two spear-heads, because she wanted to hold the uprights in her hands. She listened to the stillness and saw that a daisy had remained uncut because it grew right up against the nearest headstone. She leant her cheek against one of the uprights, indifferent to the sooty marks it would leave, and thought: the best way to remember is not to try, but to relax and let it soak in. For tomorrow she must remember this, it was essential not to make the mistake of dismissing it in the morning because of having been drunk. Being drunk made no difference: this was how *it was*. I must remember, she thought, I must remember, I must remember how beautiful it is, because now I can *see* it. It is so still, and the grass has just been cut, and the leaves are not being blown, they are just settling together, sometimes, on the air, and the wine-glass is standing on the railing, and I am alone. I am me, under the moon, on a summer night, alone. The moon is sailing slowly through the sky, and these railings are rusted under the paint so that it has flaked off in places, and if I could reach that daisy I would feel that its reddish stem is a little hairy. The wine-glass is standing there with its perfect curves and its broad foot, calm and transparent. Everything could always be like this, if only I can manage to remember.

The sound of footsteps approached the end of the passage and she jerked her head back, waiting for them to turn in after her and be Martin's. They went by, and that was all right. But since he might be following, and she was suddenly frightened at the idea of him catching up with her here, she had better go on. She took the wine-glass off the railing and

146

turned it in her fingers, thinking poor thing, tomorrow it will be no more than a slightly smeary glass which I must return to Lucy, I can't bear it. She drew back a step and stood wondering, looking at the glass, and then she began to laugh because she knew what she would do: she would leave it here. 'Goodbye, glass,' she said, holding it up towards the moon for a moment, then she threw it over the railing as hard as she could. It turned in the air, there was a tinkle as it hit a tombstone, but although she tried she could not see its fragments on the grass because it was in a shadowy patch. 'I have shattered a wine-glass against a tombstone,' she said aloud, in the light of the moon.

Walking on, out in the street again, she was jubilant and began to hum: a glass in the grass alas, a glass in the grass alas, but it was odd that those footsteps had not been Martin's. A glass in the grass, and not alas but hurrah, because at this moment nothing matters. Listen: I say to myself that I walked out on my poor love – I didn't only walk out on him, I insulted him in front of George and Lucy. He will be angry and perhaps he will mind, so that I shall soon feel bad about it – oh dear, supposing it has really . . . no I won't think of that. No, but I did this odd thing, and it doesn't matter. Here I am alone, what a relief. Perhaps it will not continue to be a relief, but that is what it is *now*.

Ah, the silly tangle of being two people – though it seemed that Martin was not much tangled, because if he had followed her straightaway he would have caught up with her by now. That florist's window, banked with fresh flowers even at night: do they take home the flowers which are beginning to fade, or do they just put them in the dustbin? So he must have gone back to his argument with George as though nothing had happened, and that, considering that he had probably forgotten her putting the keys in her purse, was pretty cool. If she was in bed by the time he got home she would pretend to be asleep – unless he started rooting about for the Alka-Seltzer: what a pity that she had left it on the kitchen dresser instead of in the bathroom, he would never find it there without help. It was tiresome to be able to see him so clearly, suddenly; she should have been a fraction more drunk, so that it would have carried her right into bed and sleep. To spoil this lovely walk by thinking of his return was a waste of time, while as for thinking of tomorrow, when he would ask her why she had done something so unlike herself . . . it was not as though he had been *very* boring, either, poor treasure; not nearly so boring as George. The best thing, the wisest thing, would be to remember poems – 'Sabrina fair, listen where thou art sitting', perhaps, or *Lycidas*, which would almost see her home.

He might have tried to run after her straight away, and have been kept there by George and Lucy against his will: perhaps a little longer between the taps might be a good thing – tap, tap, tap, tap – she could change her speed now without any special effort, but walking slowly seemed to be more tiring than walking fast.

Madeleine tried stepping on the lines between the paving-stones, then stopped and looked back, but there was only a policeman on a bicycle. He looked at her questioningly as he passed, which made him wobble. It was foolish to dawdle, better to go on briskly in an ordinary way, and perhaps, now that she had almost reached their own street, think of something everyday, such as whether they could afford Mrs Moxon three times a week instead of twice. The night was not so warm as she had thought it, but even now she was not really sorry. She was only seeing a little too clearly that soon she might be.

When, halfway along their own street, she heard first running feet on the pavement, then the chink of money in his pocket, the threat of sorriness vanished because she began to giggle at herself again, as she had done when she walked the wrong way in the square: what a fool she was, with this relief driving out her proud, private relief so immediately! In a few minutes she would have begun to be sure that he had not followed her, and if that had happened it would have been horrible: so much for her! But when he caught up, put his arms round her and pushed his face into her hair, panting, smelling of drink and gasping, 'God, darling, what made you do that?' she thought: how odd. While he was running along the road it had seemed that he, like her, would be amused, but he was not, nor was he angry. He had apparently gone off on his own into some silly fuss. He was still drunk, of course, and he was leaning on her, and he was missing the point.

'They kept saying you'd come back,' he gasped. 'And then Lucy said had you got the key, and I remembered you had, so they said that even if you didn't come back you'd be all right, and to let you cool off. But I couldn't stop thinking *in vino veritas, in vino veritas*. Madeleine, *why did you do it?*'

'Oh darling, I don't know. Don't make a fuss.'

'I'm not making a fuss, it's important.'

'It isn't important. I suppose I just felt bored, suddenly, because I was tight. I'm sorry, darling, it was just a silly thing – it doesn't matter.'

'But it might matter. You've never done anything like that before, and it's because you were tight that it might be so awful. It might be something coming out, about me!'

Oh damn, she thought. I would so like to tell him about the island and the wine-glass, but I don't see how I can. So she said, 'Come on home, sweet, and don't worry. It was nothing to do with you – absolutely not, it was to do with me. And I love you.'

'Are you sure?' said Martin.

'Yes,' said Madeleine truthfully, but feeling a little sad.

DESDEMONA

They turned into a street she had often passed but never been down, a long straight one which she supposed led to some unfamiliar part of the city. It was thick with new snow and the lamp standards on either side were tall, swan-necked, shedding a cold light.

'Where are we going?' she asked.

'To my place,' he said, 'where did you think?' But she hadn't been thinking at all, she was too drunk.

He changed down to second. 'The thing to remember,' he said, 'is the drunker I am the slower I must drive.'

She was watching the slender lamps moving slowly towards her and thinking, 'This is the street where the white lilies grow.'

There was one black figure in the street, cape, helmet, a compact conical shape. 'We'll ask him,' he said.

'Stay downwind of him,' she said, pleased with herself for this prudent thought, although there was no wind now that the snow had stopped falling. The policeman noticed nothing amiss and told them to take the first on the right, and when they did she was surprised to see that she knew where they were after all: not in an unfamiliar part of the city, but quite near the square where he'd told her he was staying.

The flat was warm and the bed had not been made for many days. She would have expected that to put her off, but now she understood that it was a good thing: sheets lying open to a warm room absorb some of the warmth and give no shock to naked bodies. But on the other hand, how could she bear a whole night in a room with no air in it? The door was open, but she could tell from the smell that the windows in the other rooms were always kept shut, so what came in was no fresher than what was there already. She might creep out of bed later and open the bedroom window just an inch – but it was his place, he liked it this way, so she mustn't be fussy. A few people had survived even in the Black Hole of Calcutta, she must remember that and concentrate on the feel of his hands and his prick: very welcome after all the tension of the evening, and how lucky that she wasn't so drunk as to feel dizzy when she lay down. Although she was too drunk, it now occurred to her, to get any real pleasure beyond a sleepy feeling that his body was an agreeable one.

Never mind, she thought when he'd rolled off her, it's not the only pleasure. This stranger with a hard face and a bit of a paunch and friendly hands and a life locked in his head so different from hers that she could imagine only corners of it; when he'd topped the ridge and slid down into helplessness in her arms, that in itself was a pleasure. She held him tenderly, one hand on the nape of his neck, one on his buttocks, and there he was at her mercy, little knowing that she was planning to creep out of bed as soon as he was thoroughly asleep and

152

open his bedroom window whether he liked it or not. That seemed to her very funny, a situation quite as delightful, for the moment, as a satisfying lovemaking would have produced. And then there was the additional pleasure of knowing that when she woke up next morning she would see this stranger walking about his room, tucking his shirt into his pants, cleaning his teeth, living his life. She'd never known a man like him before, even his snoring was interesting. And next time they'd go to her place, where she would be in control of the ventilation, and she wouldn't get so drunk.

Four months later, at her place, a moment came, as it often did now, when she knew what he was feeling. Was this true? The surer she felt that her own sensations reflected his, the more sharply she enjoyed them, so she might be wishing the correspondence. She thought this even while it was happening, but with only a fraction of her attention. Earlier, most of her mind had been following what they were doing, enjoying it, amused by it, at one moment when he hurt her rejecting it, enjoying it again; but now there was only a tiny peephole of observation left, nerve-endings had taken over from mind, communicating with each other and sending the same message out through their bodies. It must be the same message, or how could their movements be so concordant without their trying? The movements were happening, not being made. His lips were drawn back from his teeth like hers, his breath gasped like hers, the words he was moaning had the same sound as hers. Oh yes yes yes, they were together in this, they were away, they were gone ... Ah, how well they fucked together!

He liked to lie on the floor afterwards, flat on his back, arms spread, like a man crucified. She usually liked closeness after making love, but she found she enjoyed the sight of him there, dead on the carpet, his wet prick lolling on his thigh and becoming slowly smaller. It still had a little life in it. Once or twice it stirred, then sank to rest again, the silly dumb thing. She watched it through half-shut eyes and smiled. She hauled herself up, appreciating her legs' weakness, to push a pillow under his head and kiss his eyebrow, then flopped back onto the bed, belly down. She lay with blankets and sheets bundled comfortably under her torso, one arm dangling over the edge. He moved his outflung arm till their hands touched, and after their fingers had exchanged a few squeezes they remained lightly interlinked as he fell asleep.

Awake on one breath, snoring on the next: hrrr-pfff, hrrr-pfff. A gentle snore, soothing, she didn't mind it. The window was open with summer air pouring through it, and now she heard the sounds. Children were gunning each other in the gardens over which the house looked. Only the smallest boy shouted 'Bang bang', his thin voice anxious for fear he might be left behind. The others made the real sounds of every kind of gun television had ever shown them. She moved her lips silently, and knew that if she articulated the sounds they would be nowhere near so accurate. The thrush in the acacia by the wall sang on, undisturbed by the children. The permanent background of sparrow-chirps . . . a note of extraordinary mock-purity followed by a jeering whistle – a starling of course . . . someone rounding up the children . . . voices becoming distant . . . Only the birds now. The fluting thrush and the air bathing her skin, silky and warm. Only the birds and the air . . .

. . . and fingers moving between her own, a hand closing on hers. Coffee. 'What about a cup of coffee, love?' he said. Good god, they had been asleep for over an hour!

While they drank the coffee she sat on the bed and looked out of the window, and he read the *Daily Telegraph*.

'Look at it,' she said, and he turned his head in that direction and turned it back again. He didn't know the difference between an acacia and a pear tree, a thrush and a starling, because he came from another country. He might know the difference between a eucalyptus and a blue gum (or were they the same?). She gave him the benefit of that doubt, but the truth was that he didn't look at things unless he was doing something to them, and the things he did something to were usually made of metal. He knew today that the sun was shining and that it was, astonishingly, hot enough to be naked in a room with an open window, but that was all. So when she said 'Look at it,' she was only making a friendly noise at him because her body had been able to feel what his was feeling.

He, also wanting to make a friendly noise, said 'I've reached a conclusion.'

'And what conclusion have you reached?' she asked, knowing what he would answer.

'I've concluded that there's nothing better than a good fuck, excepting two good fucks.'

The first time he'd said that, she'd supposed he wanted to

start again, but now she knew it was just something he said when he was feeling good.

We might play chess? she thought. Or shall I ask him to mend the kitchen stool? She enjoyed his company when he was doing things because he took a job gravely. Watching him use his broad, short-fingered hands she felt almost as tender towards him as she did in bed. And she could still enjoy his talk about his past, listening as though she were reading a story, although now the best parts of the story had been used up. She knew the part about the captain and the first officer who both got drunk at Las Palmas, and fought, and hurt each other so badly that he, who was engineer, had to take the ship on all the way to Lisbon. She knew the part about his being reduced to shovelling grain on the docks in Sydney; the part about his running away from home at fourteen; the part about the rich old bag in Hong Kong who offered him money to sleep with her; the part where he found a big sapphire near Alice Springs and gambled it away that same night; the part where he agreed to sign on as a mercenary in the Congo and then thought better of it; the part where he bought a share in a Caribbean schooner and almost settled on St Vincent but the schooner broke up on a reef. To begin with she had felt like Desdemona listening to Othello. Looking at his box-shaped head, she had seen it as containing seas and ships and goldmines and drunken brawls in brothels and sudden emergencies and endurance and sharp wits by which he fell on his feet, and when her body felt what his felt it seemed to her that she was touching and sharing these things, and she wanted this to be true.

It was a pity that he also liked to talk about his opinions.

Twice she had let him meet friends of hers, and after that never again. Both times it began well because he came into a room well, not swaggering but suggesting swagger, inspiring curiosity and slight alarm. He didn't say much at first, and when he spoke it was factual, and his facts were as different from those of her friends as they were from hers so that, like her, the friends began by responding Desdemona-fashion. But when this first success had relaxed him he would start saying what he thought, and her friends' eyes became at first round, then cold.

It became apparent that he distrusted anything and anyone he didn't understand. Women he mistakenly didn't distrust because he thought he understood them, being able to please them in bed as he could; but any man whose experience covered different things from his own he bristled at and had to put down. If a man showed that he was well-read, then he was a dry stick; if he mentioned theatre or painting, then he was a homosexual; if he had made money, then he was a crook; if he had a social conscience, then he was an airy-fairy ninny. Any man who might, he felt, score off him had something wrong with him, except for a few he could never possibly meet and whom he elected as heroes. General Montgomery was one of these, and Franco was another (because if you knew Spain as well as he did you'd understand that without a strong man at the top . . .). When he spoke of a man with affection it always turned out that the man was safely his inferior in status or experience, some loyal and trusty peasant – but a white one. Wogs and niggers didn't count, although their women could teach some white women a thing or two. Within an hour her friends were thinking 'Has she gone mad? No doubt he's good in bed, but how could she?' That was embarrassing enough, but more painful was the spectacle of this man supposing that he was in command of the situation while in fact he was being dismissed as a stupid and disagreeable bore. All right, she too saw that he was a stupid and disagreeable bore, but with her this image was safe, she would keep it covered. These others might at any moment beam it back at him, and what would happen to him then?

She wanted to protect him because she knew the smell of his skin and the touch of his hands, and had felt his sweat and hers slippery between their bellies. But it wasn't only that. By now she had a black list – and a long one – of things to hold against him, but she also had a white list.

The white list ran:

1. He describes things well
2. He can make things with his hands
3. His mother died when he was ten and no one ever taught him anything
4. In spite of this he used to write poems when he was a boy
5. He is as scared of draughts as an old maid and has a painful corn on the little toe of his right foot
6. Before he gets out of the bath he wipes every drop off with a sponge, 'so as not to make the towel wet, of course'
7. He can make mayonnaise and he can knit.

He never bothered to explain or laugh off either his frailties or his surprising accomplishments. When he sat at her kitchen table intent on adding no more than one drop of oil at a time, or when he wore one of the two pairs of grey socks he had knitted, she almost loved him: her unselfconscious old thug.

So after those two outings they stayed at home, moving between bedroom and kitchen, sometimes playing chess, reading the papers, talking of what was under their noses like an old married couple except that they were together only two or three nights a week, not all the time. They could enjoy a movie together, but only if it happened to be a western or a thriller, and they could manage a short pub-crawl, but her natural talk over drinks was gossip about people, and he, though he would listen amiably for a while, didn't see much point in that. A decadent lot making too much fuss over nothing; that was how he saw the people she knew.

How he saw her, she didn't know. Perhaps he didn't. Whenever she told him something about herself she found herself keeping it as short as possible because he was so evidently incurious.

'What do you think of me?' she said suddenly, to the newspaper.

'You've got nice tits but you can't make pastry . . . Listen to this: "Forty-nine per cent of them came from broken homes and in almost all cases there was a history of family disturbance." Lot of nonsense.'

'Why? Who are they talking about?'

'Kids caught shop-lifting. Lot of lazy little pricks with too much pocket money and not enough grey matter to know how to use it.'

'Oh come on! Thousands of spoilt kids *don't* start stealing.'

'I had a tougher time when I was a kid than any of this lot, I bet you, and I kept straight. No – it's just a fashion, all this excuse-making for anyone who goes wrong. Any kid's lazy. Any kid'll do the soft thing rather than the hard thing, give him his own way. You just have to teach them that they can't get away with it . . . You only have to look at them in this country, now it's the fashion to let them do as they please.'

'Thank god I haven't got any,' she said, ducking an argument.

'Better touch wood there, baby! God – I remember when I was a kid, about eight or nine years old, I'd taken the old man's shotgun out into the bush behind our place one day when he'd gone into town – thought I'd get it cleaned and back onto its nails up on the wall before he ever got back. There was a little creek back there, just a slither of water with the mud like chocolate cake, and one pool left deep enough to reach to your knees. And Christ knows what happened because I was a handy kid as a rule, but there I was bang in the middle of the pool and I dropped that gun. My old man and that gun! It was a sacred object, I can tell you, so when I dropped it I panicked and began to flounder and stepped right onto it so down it went into the mud, and by the time I got it out it was choked right up with chocolate cake. So I ran for home with it – I knew it would take me hours to get it cleaned – and damn me if that day of all days he hadn't come on a neighbour who'd had an accident on the road and brought him back to our place instead of going on into town. We weren't particular about ailments, not even in my mother's day – couldn't afford to be – but after my old man had finished with me I had to stay in bed three full days, and you didn't catch me laying my hands on other people's property after that, I can tell you.'

While he was speaking she tried to imagine the look of the creek, and the skinny little boy who could handle a shotgun at eight years old, and she winced when she envisaged the kind of injury a three-days-in-bed flogging would inflict. A childhood so different from her own, a world so remote . . . but the images were pale. They were pale because she had heard this story before. She reminded herself that however often she heard it, it had still happened; his repeating himself didn't make the life contained in his head less real. But she was trying to fool herself and this time she failed: listening to him now was not like it had been at first. She reached for her nail file and caught herself thinking 'a squeezed orange'.

The words shocked her. He had taken up the newspaper again, and there were new sounds from the garden – two girls laughing. He looked comfortable on the bed with a blanket round his shoulders now the sun had gone off the window, relaxed after his good lovemaking – her good lovemaking too – and absorbed in his reading. She stared at him, then turned quickly to her mirror because although it had been disagreeable to catch those three true words in her mind, she had started to grin. It had occurred to her that Othello probably strangled Desdemona just in time.

A HOPELESS CASE

It was impossible to hear or be heard and almost impossible to move. Philip Dwight had fixed a grin on his face, but he was sure that no one could be convinced by it. A moment's genuine interest in the people round him – could they really be enjoying it, or were they just better actors than he was? – failed to distract him from his misery, and he decided that he would soon leave, whether Sarah wanted to come or not.

She wouldn't want to. He had lost sight of her, but twenty minutes ago she had been talking to a couple they knew and a friend of that couple's, a thin eager-looking man with untidy red hair and hot blue eyes. The man had been concentrating on Sarah, showing off to her, and she had been enjoying it. Philip couldn't hear her, but he knew her voice had started to sound affected. When this happened it always surprised him that instead of being put off, people laughed more than ever at what she said.

Sometimes he tried beforehand to hope that a party would be a pleasure shared, Sarah and he responding together to the people they met, or snug in a comfortable corner, watching the spectacle. She, however, saw it differently. 'But we're together all the time, darling – the whole point of going out is to talk to someone else for a change.' And she would sidle away from him into the crowd as soon as she could.

Philip began to work his way across the room to where he had last seen her, but she was no longer there. He was near the door now, he could slip out – should he slip out? He would go into the hall anyway, to draw breath and clear his head of the din.

And there in the hall was Sarah, sitting with her feet tucked up on a velvet-covered sofa which must have been moved out of the drawing-room to make space, with the red-haired man beside her. They were both talking at once, in the middle of a laughing argument. She had raised her hand to silence him. As Philip watched, the man caught her hand, pulled it down to rest on his knee and went on holding it there as he said: 'No you don't! Let me finish what I was saying.'

They hadn't noticed him. He felt as though he had been turned then and there into one of those grotesque dummies which lollop above the heads of carnival crowds, a thing stuffed with hay, its daft and tragic face hoisted in mockery and merriment. Nothing was happening – he knew that nothing was happening. Sarah on an evening out was being reminded that she was a pretty and amusing woman, that was all. He couldn't rage, he couldn't sulk, he couldn't plead, he couldn't even run away: if he did any of those things he would look – he would *be* – a fool, a carnival dummy of a *cocu imaginaire*; and he would just as certainly look a fool if he did the only thing he could reasonably do: approach them as though he had noticed nothing and say it was time to go. It wouldn't only be Sarah who would see at once that his calm was false, the man would see it too. What he was trying to hide would be coming off him like the smell of sweat, he knew it by experience. It was the situation's very triviality which made it impossible to deal with in any way that wouldn't be humiliating.

Philip had once known a humourless and pedantic Spaniard called Cristobal who was a virtuoso in jealousy. His affairs were dull for most of the time, but when, usually for no reason, he decided to be jealous a transformation took place. He would appear to grow taller, his skin would go yellow, his eyes would stare, his mouth would twist, and once he took off his belt and started slashing at the arm of a sofa, saying 'Don't let me go near her tonight, don't let me go near her or I will kill her.' He did sometimes hit his girls, or so he said, and Philip knew that he had broken all the gramophone records belonging to one of them. The girls used to be flattered to begin with, but later they would become fed up and would leave him. Cristobal recovered quickly – he knew at bottom that he would end up with a well-brought-up Spanish girl conditioned to the rules of the game – and seemed to emerge fortified from the painful but satisfying ritual of guaranteeing his masculinity, even when it lost him a girl. Philip remembered him with envy, because his own jealousy wasn't at all like that.

It was, he felt glumly, essentially rational. Why shouldn't Sarah want another man? Why, after eight years of marriage, should she be content with him? He, after all, sometimes had to think of another woman in order to make love to her convincingly. They no longer had much to talk about, he was only mildly interested in her pottery classes and her beagle puppies, and she wasn't interested at all in his work. He wasn't a smart sort of architect, his firm's factories were never illustrated in the reviews. Sarah couldn't be expected to see him as important because of his job, and in himself . . . he didn't despise himself, but there was nothing exceptional about him, nothing to keep a woman hooked. At times when he took himself to task for his jealousy – times when it was inactive – he always ended with a bleak sense that it wasn't so silly as it seemed.

But Sarah insisted that it was silly. The other day her old beagle bitch had been off her food, and she had called him into the kitchen and said, 'Look – I want you to watch this.' She put the dish of food down in its usual place and started to cajole the bitch: 'Amber, come on Amber sweetie, come and eat your lovely dinner', and Amber stayed in her basket. Then Sarah went to the window, leant out and called the other dogs: 'Topaz! Jasper! Come on, din-dins!' and Amber instantly sat up, got out of the basket, went to the dish and began furiously to eat, her hackles up. Philip had laughed, thinking Sarah had wanted him to watch only because it was amusing, but she had silenced him by giving him a wry look and saying 'Don't you realise *that's you*?'

No, he couldn't put on his feeble act of not minding what he had seen. He had already backed into the drawing-room again, and turning round he came face to face with Lilian Morris.

'Lilian!' he said. 'Look, if you happen to see Sarah will you tell her I've bolted. I can't find her, and anyway I don't want to drag her away, but I can't stick any more of this.'

'Neither can I,' said Lilian. 'I'm just leaving – wait a moment, I saw Jenny Boyd a second ago, she'll tell Sarah.'

Taking his hand, she dragged him up to Jenny Boyd so that he had no alternative to repeating his message. And Lilian, he was thinking meanwhile, having just seen him coming in from the hall, would know that he had been lying when, on the way out, she saw Sarah there. . . . But to his relief a group of people had collected, concealing the sofa.

'Delicious air!' said Lilian as they left the house. 'I'll say this for an overcrowded party, it makes you appreciate breathing.'

'And hearing and thinking and seeing and feeling,' said Philip, bound by the situation to play up his discomfort in the crowd. 'I'm glad you wanted to leave too. I was beginning to think I'd become a freak in my old age – everyone else seemed to be having a good time.'

'*No one* could have been having a good time at that party,' said Lilian. 'Really! I know the temptation to polish off all one's friends at one go, but if Jake and I can resist it, they ought to be able to do the same.'

'Where is Jake? Have you left him there like I've left Sarah?'

'Oh no – I doubt if I could have got him there. No, he's had to go to Exeter, poor lamb, to sort out the affairs of an old aunt of his who died last month.'

They had started to walk away from the corner of the square most likely to produce taxis, and Philip stopped. 'Wait a minute,' he said, 'I think I'm going the wrong way. We didn't bring the car so I must catch a cab to my underground station.'

'I've got my car, it's parked just round this corner. Can't I give you a lift?'

The Dwights lived in Highgate, the Morrises in Kensington, so Philip could only accept a lift as far as he would have taken a cab, but it would give him another ten minutes or so in company and he felt better in company than alone. He couldn't obliterate his own absurdity, but he could glimpse it obliquely instead of facing it. To make a fuss about nothing was bad enough, and when the fuss might easily turn nothing into something. . . . Supposing Sarah was tempted by the red-haired man, she could have done nothing about it if Philip had stayed there; while now she had both an opportunity and a booster of justifiable annoyance towards grabbing that opportunity. And if, on the other hand, she hadn't found the man attractive, being left in the lurch like this would almost certainly make her overlook it and accept an invitation to dine with him; and then, in a fury with Philip, and having drunk a good deal. . . .

'Are you heading for anything?' he asked Lilian. 'Because if not, why don't we have dinner together?'

'What a nice idea. All I was heading for was a boiled egg and early bed.'

It was Sarah's insensitivity which baffled Philip. If it was true that she didn't want anyone else, why did she behave as though she did? She insisted that his distress was neurotic, but neurotic pain is as bad as any other kind, she knew that, so even if she was right, and there was nothing to reassure him about, it was cruel of her to withhold reassurance. How could she love him if she wasn't prepared to sacrifice a few small treats for her vanity (that's what she said they were) for his peace of mind? Why, out of all that mob, did she have to pick an apparently unattached man with hot eyes?

They went to a small Italian restaurant and when they were settled at their table it occurred to Philip that Lilian was looking her best. Sarah laughed at her for overdressing, saying that she could be trusted to put a piece of costume jewellery on any part of her anatomy which couldn't be exposed, but this evening she was glittering less than usual, and although Sarah would certainly think her dress too low-cut for a six-to-eight drinks party, what it exposed was pleasing. She had a dark skin which looked as though it would smell spicy, and although he usually thought of her expressive brown eyes as funny – she used them a lot as she talked, rolling them and even, when she was clowning, squinting them – he noticed now how friendly they were. It seemed to give her pleasure to look at him.

The two couples had met on a skiing holiday and discovered that they had the husbands' work and several acquaintances in common. They hadn't built much on the cheerful intimacy of that first fortnight, but it had been enough to make them feel like friends when they happened to meet, and they asked each other to dinner from time to time. Philip and Lilian had never been alone together.

He didn't know what to say to her. He'd asked after her two children in the car, and they'd done 'Where did you go this summer?' – Jake's aunt – relations in general . . . swapping guilts and resentments about families was usually a good bet. But Lilian, surprisingly, turned out to have no guilts or resentments to swap. 'No,' she said, 'mine are honeys. I suppose there'll be worries when one of them dies and leaves the other stranded, but I don't think it'll be a burden. Parents are only people, after all. It always puzzles me, the way 'parents' – and 'children' too, for that matter – are talked about as though they were a separate species. They're only people who've got old or people who are still young. I don't suppose God sees any difference between them and us.'

'God? Are you a believer?'

'No, but I mean if there was something up there looking at us from a god's-eye viewpoint, I'm sure he – or perhaps it's she! – would be amused by all these little identical ant-like beings imagining distinctions between them. I mean, it would probably be quite difficult to have one's widowed mother in the house, but it's not all that easy to have a husband or wife there, is it?'

'I suppose it isn't.'

'In fact it seems to me that if one can cope with marriage one ought to be able to cope with any other relationship standing on one's head.'

She spoke so easily that Philip quickly suppressed the question: were Lilian and Jake having a bad time? She was meaning it only in a general sense, of course, but it shocked him slightly. The only difficult thing about his own marriage, surely, was the possibility – his silly imagining of the possibility – that Sarah might take another man.

'Look,' said Lilian, resting her chin on her hand and beaming curiosity and interest full into his eyes – hers really were enormous: 'Look, you and Sarah have no children, so you know more about marriage in its pure state, so to speak, than I do. What about it do *you* think makes it worthwhile?'

Good god, but she was different when you got her alone! She'd never talked like this at dinner parties. She was leaning forward, and the dusky cleft between her breasts. . . .

'I suppose,' he said, 'having one person in one's life whom one can depend on – one person who really does know you, and whom you really know.'

'Not being looked after?'

'Oh really, Lilian! I didn't know you were such a cynic.'

'No, but just think. Try to imagine getting up in the morning and finding all your shirts and socks and underpants dirty, and knowing they'd go on being dirty unless *you* did something about it. And that every time you wanted to eat, *you* had to decide what to get and then make the meal yourself. Don't you think that not having to bother about things like that may be one of the most important things in marriage for you, even if you never think about it? I'm sure it is with Jake.'

'What about sex?' said Philip, although all he'd meant to do was avoid answering a silly question.

'Oh sex – well, yes, what the books always say about familiar sex being different but still cosy is true, I suppose, but do you really think cosiness is worth more than excitement? I love snuggling up with Jake, but I sometimes have to think of someone else to work myself up to it.'

What Philip thought was, 'She's had too much to drink.' What his voice said was, 'So do I.'

'There you are, then,' said Lilian, sitting back with the satisfaction of someone who has won a point. 'The snuggling up part is nice, but it doesn't amount to a reason for the institution. The being looked after part might – and the looking after, because most women enjoy it. But mostly I think married people are just *propping each other up*.'

'But people need propping up.'

'Well, they shouldn't.'

'Why not? Look –' and he broke off. If he went on he'd tell too much. And why should he let her get away with this aggressiveness? Her manner was cheerful and relaxed, but it *was* aggressiveness. He would take the initiative.

'It sounds to me,' he said, 'as though you and Jake were going through one of those bad spells.'

'Oh no, darling. Jake and I are fine – we got our bad spells over long ago. We have an agreement now. We've got the children, and we like each other very much, so we stick together, but we go our own ways. We observe the decencies, of course – I'd be furious if Jake flaunted an affair under my nose, but he'd never dream of doing that – and we're as happy together as we've ever been.'

'I don't believe that.'

'Why not?'

'It's not natural. You can't possibly not mind.'

'Now that's a maddening habit, telling people what they feel or don't feel –' but before Philip could apologise she had switched her mood, and she went on '– though you're right in a way, of course. It is rather sad, giving up dreams of happy-ever-after-with-my-only-love – one would *like* it to be possible. I expect I'd have gone on pretending if Jake had let me, and it might have gone on feeling real, too, because then I'd never have had a flutter myself.'

'What do you mean?'

'Well, you see, I felt like you to begin with, when it was Jake fluttering and me sitting at home forlorn – how *could* I not mind when he was destroying what I lived for, and all that. But when things started happening to *me*. . . .' and she threw back her head and laughed out with such genuine amusement that people turned to look at her and started to smile in sympathy. 'Oh god!' she said. 'Aren't human beings awful, aren't they absurd? The *things* one catches oneself out in!'

'You're an extraordinary woman,' said Philip. She seemed at this moment slightly larger than life, her eyes and teeth gleaming in laughter, orange reflections from the shaded lights on her cheekbones and forehead, and the slight cushions of flesh swelling above the rim of her dress giving an almost imperceptible jelly-like quiver which made him salivate. 'I never realised before,' he said, 'what an extra-ordinary woman you are.'

'What was your first impression of me, that time in Kitzbuhel?'

'A mother. You were taking the children off to the nursery slopes and you had that rather daunting sort of calm resourcefulness about you that good mothers have. I thought you probably cooked very well, and said the right things to Jake's partners, but that what you were most concerned with was your children.'

'I am a good mother, and I do cook well.'

'I know that – and then in the evening it was surprising when you started to take someone off and I saw you were a clown as well.' He naturally didn't add that he and Sarah had also seen that when she was free of the discipline of skiing clothes she could look like a barmaid. That's what Sarah had said, but now it seemed to Philip that his own assent had been superficial, and that if he had paid more attention to Lilian at the time it would have been other things that he would have noticed.

'What was your impression of me?' he asked.

'I thought you didn't know you were good-looking, which was nice, and that your manners were too good so that you might be concealing some quite creepy thoughts, which wasn't so nice.'

'Creepy?'

'Well, critical – ironic. Or anyway not showing what you were really feeling, like at the party this evening. I saw you earlier and there you were, smiling away so attentively at someone, and really all you were longing to do was bolt.'

It was an acceptable image compared to the reality, and Philip adopted it. Anxiety and tension had fallen away and he began enjoying Lilian instead of watching her, and talking well. He hadn't talked so amusingly for a long time. It was like riding a bicycle, he thought vaguely; however long you don't do it, you don't lose the knack. Between them there started to be that curious suspension of awareness which means that if you chose to be aware you would know what was going to happen next.

And it did, too, as smoothly as though this were a fantasy. Neither of Philip's two other infidelities had been so simple. It wasn't late when they finished dinner, and coffee at Lilian's place rather than in the restaurant would be so obviously more agreeable that there was no undercurrent to deciding on it. The babysitter lived near and didn't have to be driven home; the children had gone to bed and to sleep early. While Lilian was tucking them in – checking on them? – it was more the sexiness of the situation than thoughts of her which began to excite Philip: the silence in her living-room, the dim light – she had switched on only one lamp – the smell of the Roman hyacinths planted in a wide copper pan, the width of the sofa, the intimate sound of the clock's ticking. It was a pretty little French clock, cleverly placed to look surprising but decorative in what was evidently an architect's room. There was altogether more softness and ornament about than is usual in such a room, but it was used well; either Jake was boss, or Lilian had better taste in rooms than she had in clothes.

She came in with the coffee on a tray and went across to the drinks table, where she stood with her back to him, raising a bottle of brandy to the light to see if there was any left in it. 'And why not?' he thought as he went over and put his hands on her shoulders. 'Why not, for god's sake, after all I've gone through?'

It was her heat which made his own flare up so violently. By the time they were on the sofa and she was opening his fly she was panting and giving little moans, and he had an erection such as he hadn't had for years; he had that real tipped-over-the-edge, nothing-could-stop-me-now feeling, and hardly noticed her body's feel, taste and smell so urgently did he need to get into her. She used words. 'Screw me,' she muttered, 'fuck me, drive it in, drive it in deep,' and opening his eyes, seeing her face lost to everything but sensation, he was carried dizzily into coming much sooner than he wanted to. But either she was as quick as he, or she was a generous faker: she was there with him, or so it seemed, and had turned herself into a blissful feather-bed.

Only a few minutes after Philip's prick had slipped out of the wet warmth where he wished it could stay for ever, the clock on the chimney piece gave a tinkling chime and struck ten. He counted idly, half asleep, then did a double-take: ten – and he had to get back to Highgate no later than he would have done if he'd just had dinner out. Sarah was going to be angry enough already – if, that is, she herself had got back to Highgate. . . .

'I'll call a minicab,' said Lilian. 'You can wash in the downstairs loo if you want to – look, across there. Don't worry, love, it won't take long to get back at this time in the evening.' Still disheveled and flushed, but calm and kind. Sweet Lilian, he was going to have to think about her later, see her again somehow, get her properly into bed, but now it was only by deliberate self-discipline that he could stroke her hair off her face, kiss her and say the right things. When he was in the loo he must wash himself carefully and make sure that there weren't any marks on his trousers. Luckily she hadn't been wearing scent. . . .

She said as he left that the best time to telephone her was between ten and eleven in the morning. 'It won't be easy, but it would be nice to meet again, don't you think?' The words were brisk but the voice was husky. 'Yes I do think – of course I do,' he said; and in the cab he felt marvellous: comfortably distanced from Sarah, restored, in control, immune. Anxiety at the thought of finding the house empty began to niggle halfway through the drive, but when he saw a light in their bedroom confidence returned. It would only be a quarrel, not disaster. Sarah knew that he really did detest that sort of drinks party, so it wouldn't be incredible that this evening he had flipped and gone off in a temper when he couldn't immediately find her, and he'd tell her he'd eaten with the Morrises. The nearer a lie came to the truth, the better. Lilian might well have left the party early in order to pick Jake up somewhere.

The dogs came to greet him. Sarah hadn't yet shut them up for the night in the back passage, their 'bedroom' – no, of course not, it was still quite early. She was only upstairs herself because she was annoyed. Philip liked his house. Going up the stairs he was aware of the carpet under his feet – they'd just bought it and scrapped the old one given them by Sarah's mother – and noticed the shadows thrown on the ceiling by the white paper lampshade he'd designed himself. As he always did when relaxed, he enjoyed the vermilion chest under the window on the landing. It was a pity that Sarah was going to be angry, but it was nice to be home.

He opened the bedroom door. She wasn't there – must be in the bathroom, yes, he could hear her – but the dress she'd been wearing was over the back of a chair, her bag and gloves were on the bed and her shoes were by the dressing-table, one of them lying on its side. She was very cross indeed; she hardly ever failed to put things away as she took them off. But the familiar room was welcoming. There would be no point in going downstairs again – it was always Sarah who put the dogs to bed – so he might as well start undressing while she was in the bathroom.

And suddenly Philip realised that the sound of running water wasn't made by the taps of the hand-basin, but by those of the bath. They were full on, both of them. Sarah was running a bath. She had come home, hurried upstairs, stripped off her clothes and gone straight to take a bath: she, who always had her bath in the morning except when she took one before going out to a party, which she had done this evening.

Slowly he pushed his arm back into the sleeve of his jacket, feeling his ribs shake as his heart began to thump. He mustn't – he couldn't – be there when she came into the bedroom pink-faced, smelling only of soap and talcum powder. He must go downstairs. A drink – yes, he must get himself a drink, that was what one did.

He went to the kitchen because it was the room furthest from the bedroom. There was no anger yet, only pain. He observed it with dim interest: he couldn't describe it, but it

was a perfectly distinct pain, like a physical wound. Pain and grief. Pain and fear. Panic, perhaps. He sat at the kitchen table staring straight in front of him, feeling this sensation swell within him and not even thinking of asking himself why it should do so.

BURIED

Colonel Cooper and Mrs Klein, brother and sister, forty-eight and forty-six years old, were driving too fast down a lane in Essex on a moonlit night in May.

'You're going too fast,' said Mrs Klein.

'Balls,' said Colonel Cooper. He was a man who rarely used bad language, she a woman who hardly ever did, but when they were together (which was not often) it was curious how they would sometimes speak quite coarsely.

It was two years since Mrs Klein had last visited Guy Cooper and his wife. She liked their home – it had been hers, too, until she grew up – and she was glad that Guy kept it going now that he had retired. But on her last visit her husband had come with her and she had sworn, as she had done so many times: never again. Guy had not been rude and Harry Klein had not been bored; it had only been for a weekend and anyway the Coopers fascinated him. But Enid Klein had known her brother's thoughts as clearly as though he had spoken them and she could not endure to see Harry in a room where such thoughts were going on.

'Well, it's your life,' Guy had said twenty years ago, soon after their father died. He was staying in her London flat for a night on his way home for leave. 'If you like it I suppose it's all right, but it seems bloody unwholesome to me. No air, no green, nothing but stink and racket' (that had been his picture of London since he was a boy) 'and those long-haired friends of yours, all talk, no action, natter natter natter on subjects they know nothing about. If you go on like this you'll end by marrying some frightful Commie Yid.'

'That's just what I am going to do, if you want to know,' Enid had answered. 'Except that he's a Socialist, but I wouldn't expect you to know the difference.'

'Good God!' he had said. 'Not really? You mean you've actually got engaged to one?'

'I'm marrying Harry Klein next month – the economist.'

'*Really?*' he had said, not sure whether she was pulling his leg. When she had convinced him, he flushed; but whether with embarrassment at his own gaffe or with anger she was not sure. Whichever it was, he drowned it in a guffaw. 'My God!' he roared. 'It's too good to be true, it's just what I've always said would happen. Christ! Think of Mama and the uncles!'

Enid and Guy hardly had a thought in common but they had this way out: this ribaldry. He was putting Harry, she knew, on a level with his own disreputable bachelor affairs of which he could always tell her and at which she would laugh. Once he had seduced a sad girl in Enid's spare room and Enid, seeing him a monster, had laughed till she cried at his account of it. It was she, on that occasion, who had saved something by summoning up the faces of Mama and the uncles.

'I've already told Mama,' she had said. 'You'll find her wearing her expression of doom, but she'll get used to it.'

'I suppose we'll all have to,' said Guy; then, pulling himself together (they had gone separate ways for so long, he did not much care): 'You've always known what you wanted. I expect you're right and he's the chap for you. Anyway, E, I hope you'll be very happy.' And away he went, out of her life again, to tell his friends, when he thought of it, 'And now my Red sister is marrying some frightful Jew.'

Mama had become fond of Harry. He was amusing and distinguished, neither over-rich nor disagreeable to look at. Even the uncles had come to accept him, although they still made a point of bringing his career and position into any conversation with strangers as soon as possible: 'A remarkably brilliant chap, of course,' they would always say. And Guy, who hardly ever saw him, would not have said he disliked him. It was just that his courtesy was over-careful; that under his moustache, Enid knew, there was the suppressed twitch of a knowing grin. By common consent he and Harry would avoid politics, which meant that to keep talk going Harry had to spend a lot of time being interested in Guy's affairs. He genuinely wanted to know about farming – he always wanted to know about things – and his questions were sensible, but the fact that he had to ask them was to Guy conclusive evidence that the chap *had no idea*. He knew his stuff in his own field, Guy didn't doubt that, and he had never done anything disgraceful that anyone knew of: but he said 'revoalve' instead of 'revolve' and Guy was sure that he would wear galoshes on a muddy day, throw up if he saw maggots in a sheep's flesh and would not know how to talk to the men. All of which was true. Guy himself sometimes paddled about in absurd overshoes of rubberised felt, fastening over the instep with a latchet and known in the family as 'Jemimas'. It was not easy to see in what way they were more correct than galoshes, but it was partly Enid's own sensitivity to the latter which had made her so detest their visits to the Coopers.

'You're a freak, darling,' Harry used to tell her in the days before they had become too accustomed to the situation to think about it. 'There must have been a scandal in your family's past that's coming out in you. Do you think one of the Barbados Coopers legitimised a little coloured bastard, or an Essex one took a gypsy girl by *droit de seigneur* and adopted the baby? I can't conceive how civilised thinking crept in otherwise.' He had never expected her to quarrel with her family, partly because he was too intelligent to mind their attitude, partly because, with all his intelligence, he was not quite able to comprehend its full depths under the sufficiently amiable surface they presented to him. Enid could comprehend it, though, and she often wondered why she had not quarrelled, or not for long. 'Yes,' she had said. 'A raped slave girl would explain why I hate them so much – that poor girl's blood boiling in my veins!' For it was with hatred, sometimes, that she came away from encounters dictated by habit, good nature and affection.

This May, Harry was in New York for a conference. Guy's wife, Lavender, wrote once a year to Enid, saying 'When are you coming to see us?' and nostalgic for a country spring,

Enid had taken this chance of doing so. Now Lavender was in bed with a migraine and Guy and Enid had been without her to dine with neighbours. Back they were driving, much too fast, over a surface left greasy by a light shower.

'Guy, please!' said Enid.

'You're becoming a fusser,' said Guy.

'Well of course, old age,' she was answering when they came to a bend, Guy cut it too sharply, the car bumped the verge, swayed onto the crown of the road and went into a skid. There were some long, suspended moments while Guy was all his hands on the wheel, concentrating too sharply to think, playing the skid, and Enid was saying to herself in what seemed a calm, slow voice: 'So here we go at last, as long as it isn't that oak tree, head on. . . .' Then, with a crunch, they fetched up, bonnet obliquely into the right-hand bank, less violently than Guy deserved.

Enid was jolted forward out of her seat. She was on the floor, Guy on top of her, for he had twisted sideways at the last moment in case the steering shaft should be driven backwards. Neither was hurt, but Enid could feel a ladder in her stocking running deliberately the whole length of her left leg.

'You fool,' she mumbled into her own sleeve. 'You've laddered my stocking.'

'You all right?'

'How can I tell with you on top of me?'

They disentangled themselves, Enid got out and Guy betrayed himself shaken by staying where he was, starting the engine again and trying to back the car without first seeing what damage had been done. A grinding sound and a shudder were all he got.

'I can't see properly,' called Enid, 'but one of the headlights is out and there's glass all over the road and I should think your bumper and your right wing are sort of wrapped round that wheel.'

Guy swore, edged out of the passenger's seat, put his hand on her shoulder and said he was sorry.

'I should hope you are, we're lucky not to be dead. What do we do now? How far from home are we?'

'Three miles by the road. Only about three-quarters if we cut across country – oh, your shoes and things.'

'Isn't there somewhere nearer where we can telephone the garage?'

'Only Longmeadow, and I'm not going to knock *Croft* up.'

'Why not?'

'Perfectly bloody man.'

Enid remembered talk of a feud developing: of a newcomer who last winter had lured Guy's pheasants into his own coverts, had drained a field in such a way as to turn part of one of Guy's meadows into a bog, had encouraged ('I saw him with my own eyes!') his heifers to break out into Guy's oats, had shot at Lavender's corgi when he found it on his land. The other side of the story she had not heard, but Guy was a friendly man on his own ground, and she was prepared to believe that Mr Croft was mad.

They stood there in the lane, the car still ticking gently in the right-hand bank, a nightingale chuckling in the depths of the wood which shadowed them on the left.

'If we go through that wood,' said Guy, 'we'd only have his sixteen-acre field between us and Croft's house. We could go through his yard and then there's the cart-track running down the hill that comes out on our road – you know, by the big walnut tree. Look, the best thing will be for you to get back into the car and I'll go through Croft's and telephone Beckett to send his breakdown van. Then I'll come and fetch you in the truck.'

'No,' said Enid. 'I'll come with you.'

'You'll muck up your shoes.'

'Never mind, they're quite old and the heels aren't high, I can't wear high heels any more.'

'You're sure?'

'Yes, of course. Let's go.'

She did not particularly want to walk, but Guy's assumption that she would be awkward in the country always annoyed her, brought up as she had been as deep in it as he was. Deeper, indeed, for he was sent away to school earlier, and for much longer. Also she did not like the prospect of sitting alone in that dark lane, for the trees overhung it, the moonlight was only able to make darkness more profound and disturbingly mobile round the edges.

'A pity it's not still the Harpers up at Longmeadow,' she said, taking the cigarette Guy offered her. She was surprised that her hand was shaking. She was feeling rather bold and free, the mood after a near thing in which people make jokes in loud voices.

'Yes. Do you remember old Pincher harrying their pigs?' answered Guy, and they both laughed.

They walked back down the lane some twenty yards to where there was a gate into a ride. It was padlocked and had a defensive bristle of brushwood wired to its top rail. 'The silly ass,' said Guy. 'Just the sort of thing he would do – and a gap here beside the post anyone could get through. Careful. I'll hold this back – keep your head down and watch out for brambles.'

'Lord!' said Enid. 'It's a long time since I did anything like this. Thirty years or more, it must be.' She clutched her full skirt to her stomach, bent almost double and pushed through the gap, twigs pulling at her hair and drops scattering. 'It's not too wet,' she said once through. 'Not boggy.'

'You wait,' said Guy.

They began to walk through the wood, speaking little and in hushed voices. Among the trees the night became positive, not an absence of day but a world to which Enid was a native returning after long absence. The nightingale sang louder at their approach and she remembered that they did it to warn off enemies. She remembered that, and she remembered the small sounds that come out of a wood at night, the sense of creatures moving back into shadow to watch intruders. It startled her to find the strangeness so familiar.

Guy had fallen into his countryman's long, slow stride. When she could distinguish the set of his head and shoulders she saw that he was withdrawn and alert, automatically the hunter. As a boy he had boasted that he could find his way about any wood in the neighbourhood as easily in darkness as by day, and it had been true.

'Do you still go out at nights?' she asked; and he, remembering the times to which she was referring, said, 'Of course not – though I sometimes wish I did. One grows soft.'

Soon they came to the wet patches he had foretold and their feet sucked: Enid felt water running in under her instep, then her right foot went deep, came up shoeless and was groping, only to sink bare in soft mud.

'Oh bugger!' she exclaimed and Guy laughed.

'Hold on,' he said. 'Don't move, or we'll lose it. I'll light a match.' She stood with her stockinged foot in the mud and felt relaxed: once really wet, why worry?

'I'm terribly sorry, E,' said Guy. 'I warned you, you should have stayed in the car.'

'I think I'm rather enjoying this,' she said, watching his grey head in the light of the match as he stooped to pick up the shoe.

The gate out of the wood on Croft's side was not locked. They came into a big field under grass, sloping up to where the trees and roofs of the farm made a dark outline. It seemed very light after the wood, dangerously exposed.

'Which was worse in the war?' asked Enid. 'On night patrols, I mean. Being in the open when they could see you easily but so could you see them, or being in thick cover so that you might stumble on them at any minute?'

'The open, every time,' he answered. 'It wasn't logical, I suppose, there was just as much danger in a wood or among buildings, but you wanted to feel hidden, like an animal. I wouldn't fancy coming out here into the moonlight if there were a lot of Jerries in the orchard up there, or behind us.'

'Did you do it often?' she asked in a subdued voice, glancing back at the wood in which men could so easily be lying on their bellies, perhaps shifting a little to avoid uncomfortable roots, one of them reaching out to hold down a branch in the hedge (she could feel the lichened bark against her fingers) the better to watch her and Guy.

'Pretty often, at one time,' he said gruffly.

She noticed that as he walked he had begun to turn his head slowly from side to side and she found herself doing it too, watching for movement.

'We'll go round these bullocks,' he murmured. 'We don't want them careering about and bringing someone to see what's wrong.' Enid, for all her peering, had not seen that the patches of deeper shadow ahead were cattle, lying down.

They circled the animals quietly and came to the fence between the field and Mr Croft's orchard.

'We follow this fence,' said Guy, 'and then we have to go through the yard, right under the back windows of the house. Keep behind me. I want to make sure there's no one about.'

'Is there a dog?' she whispered.

'Yes, but I think he keeps it indoors at night.'

'It wouldn't really matter if he caught us. He couldn't do anything.'

'He's not going to catch us.'

Guy was back on night patrol, she realised, and enjoying himself. How could he enjoy it when he had gone through gates like that and known that Germans really might be lying in wait? Enid knew that she could never do it if it were real, she simply *could* not. She was smiling at the thought, but the back of her neck prickled and the palms of her hands were damp.

When they were still some yards from the gate, 'Wait!' muttered Guy, and stopped so abruptly that she bumped him. He reached back, clutched her arm and dug in his fingers so hard that it hurt. She froze. At first she could only hear a little owl, back in the wood, then she heard voices. Footsteps were coming across the yard, two men were talking, the yellow light of a hurricane lantern was bobbing.

'Guinea, we'd better call out,' she whispered, but she could not have moved. The steps came nearer, the chain on the gate rattled, and 'Get down!' snapped Guy.

'Oh nonsense,' she was going to say, but she had done it. She was lying in wet grass beside him, her lace frock and her best coat huddled under her, a thistle brushing her cheek. 'Now we're trapped – now we *can't* be caught,' she thought, panic-struck – for how to explain such a posture on the part of two formally dressed middle-aged people in the dead of night, on someone else's premises? It could not be done.

The men had stopped on the other side of the gate. Very cautiously Guy moved until his head was near Enid's. 'Cow calving, I expect,' he whispered.

'Lunatic!' she whispered back, and felt him shake with laughter, then catch his breath as the chain rattled again. One of the men must have had his hand on it.

'She'll do till morning,' an old man's voice was saying.

'I don't like the looks of that discharge,' said the other voice. 'Still, she's in good condition, if she gets rid of it tonight she'll come to no harm. You'd better get along home now

– and don't forget, I want George to take the tractor down to Beckett's tomorrow, so tell him to come and see me first thing.'

'He can bring back them iron rails while he's about it,' said the first voice. Then: 'Good night, don't wake the missus.'

'Good night.'

One set of footsteps started off across the yard, the gate was opened by the other man.

'Guinea . . .' breathed Enid.

'Sh . . . keep your face down,' and Guy, who was farthest from the hedge, wriggled closer so that they were both well inside the deepest shadow. The gate creaked shut, a man coughed and spat, then walked away obliquely across the field. Guy raised his head to watch him go.

'All clear,' he said when the man had vanished, getting to his feet. He helped Enid up and tweaked at her coat, the skirt of which had caught up on one side. 'Well, old E,' he said, 'what would your London friends have thought if they'd seen you just now?'

'God knows,' she answered, giggling. 'For goodness' sake let's get out of this.'

'Just a minute.' Guy moved away a couple of steps, turned towards the hedge and in a moment she could hear that he was urinating. 'As though we were still children,' she thought, then suddenly wondered: 'Why on earth did we never go back to see if the chestnuts were still there?'

When Guy was eight, about to go to school for the first time – preparatory school, to be followed by public school, to be followed by Sandhurst, to be followed by the army: the last time she was with him, really – he had managed to come out with German measles on the day term began. It gave them a reprieve of almost two autumn weeks. They had never collected so many horse-chestnuts before. They buried them in a rotten tree stump, clawing out handfuls of cottony wood to make damp, nestlike places into which they stuffed the nuts. 'The soft wood will make them keep,' Guinea had told her as they packed it back. 'We must make it look as if there was nothing here so that no one will find them.' They had stored away their treasure, sure that when he came back from school they would find the chestnuts still glossy, still theirs. She remembered it as a secret occasion, sad, full of the physical ache of the nostalgia which, in the days before they had lost anything, they could induce at will. Once, when they were away from home, Guy had said: 'When I hear a cuckoo I think terribly of the water meadow,' and she had listened to the cuckoo and seen what he meant. 'Cuckoo, cuckoo, cuck . . .' and her heart would turn over with longing. After that they could both bring tears into their own eyes by listening to the cuckoo in the right way, and they had buried the chestnuts on a day when that feeling was about.

They had taken him away to school soon afterwards. 'Did I miss him?' she wondered now, following him silently through Mr Croft's yard, under the house in which one upstairs window showed a light. A horse stamped behind a stable door. She could remember nothing of her feelings but she must have missed him, she supposed. Had they not lived entirely together? 'Squirrels, moles?' she thought suddenly. Scurrying secretly among the branches or the roots of the adult life going on about them. They had slept in the same room, washed in the same bath water, stolen the same fruit, shared the telling of the same stories, loved the same dog, plotted death for a French governess with the same hatred. She had known his terror of wolves; he, her horror of darkness. Equally inquisitive, they had explored old machinery in barns, examined each other's genitals in a loft. They both knew that water was the loveliest thing, that red was a colour you wanted to eat. Not even with Harry, she thought, not even in her long deep love, such intimacy. . . . Before they took him away Guy was sick – she remembered that. Before he was properly in the car he had to get out of it again to be sick, but they drove him off. All of the family had known that he was never anything but desperate with unhappiness at school, but no one had questioned that he must be there. And what had she felt about it? When he had returned for the holidays, misery had already begun to make him a different person, and she had been busy with cousins.

Walking down the cart-track to the road they returned to good sense.

'I don't think I'll bother to ring Beckett's until the morning,' said Guy. 'They won't answer at this hour. Will you mind going to the station in the truck? I can order a car if you like.'

'Don't be silly, of course I won't mind. But that's the last time I'll drive with you unless Lavender is there. I can feel a bruise coming up on my elbow and my coat's stiff with mud.'

'It'll brush off.'

He had written a poem when he was at his prep school, she remembered. She had come across it much later, when she was about fourteen, and he, then sixteen, had laughed it off. It was a long poem about being at home. She knew its last lines:

The blackbird bounced so that the leaves shook.
There was a rabbit under every wheat stook.
I told Pincher to catch a rabbit
But he had a bad habit
Of barking loudly to give them warning.
Then I woke up and it was a winter night
But I had thought it was a dewy morning.

'We deserve a whisky,' said Guy as they let themselves into the house, and they drank one in the dining-room, talking comfortably enough until he said: 'Give Harry our love when he gets back. What's he up to now? Encouraging a lot of wretched niggers to stick their necks out?'

Enid told him coldly, and for the second time, the purpose of Harry's conference, then went upstairs. Her beautiful blue hair, she found, was sticking out like a mad wig, and her dress was torn in two places.

An hour later she dreamt that she was running across grass, Guy with her, then he was gone. She turned to see what had become of him and there were two men in uniform crouching over something stretched on the ground. Curious and happy, she ran back saying, 'What have you got there?' – and it was Guy. One of the men half rose and turned towards

her, eyes staring, but the other crouched lower over Guy, one hand on his throat, the other clamped over his mouth. When she saw what they were doing the scream of horror jolted out of her, waking her. She lay there, hearing her own voice as it moaned, 'Poor little boy. Oh poor, poor little boy.'